PR 9499.3.D4
DHI

From

D0994206

The Wo[...]
34 Great Sutton [...]

Leena Dhingra was born in India, but came to Europe as a small child, following Partition in 1947. She has lived in France, England, Belgium and India, and has worked in the theatre, as a film technician, as a publicity officer and as a teacher.

She contributed to the anthology *Watchers and Seekers* (The Women's Press, 1987), and has had stories published in magazines in India and in Britain. This is her first novel.

She lives in London with her daughter.

LEENA DHINGRA

Amritvela

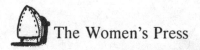 The Women's Press

First published by The Women's Press Ltd 1988
A member of the Namara Group
34 Great Sutton Street, London EC1V 0DX

British Library Cataloguing in Publication Data available

Typeset by MC Typeset, Chatham, Kent
Printed and bound in Great Britain by
Hazell Watson & Viney Ltd, Aylesbury, Bucks

Amritvela – the time of nectar,
the time just before dawn
when the sun has risen but cannot as yet be seen.

To my mother, Kamala, for her stories, and my father, Baldoon, for his poetry – which lives on in me. All my love and thanks.

One

The non-stop flight to New Delhi is now halfway. But only my watch informs me of that. Through the window we appear quite immobile, suspended over a vast expanse of curdling clouds. If, as I have often said, I feel myself to be suspended between two cultures, then this is where I belong, the halfway mark. Here in the middle of nowhere, up in the atmosphere, is my space – the halfway point between East and West. My watch informs me and my mind agrees.

The plane is quite full. Families with children, husbands and wives, and a few alone, like me. Most of them are Indians, from America, Canada, England. Are they visiting? Or returning home? What am I doing? Who knows! But here, on a plane, in my space – I feel safe . . .

Safe! Eleven years old and walking down Piccadilly on my own I felt safe. It was my first time in London, but I felt quite safe. 'I'm in Piccadilly now so I can't go to jail because the lowest the double dice can turn is two!' And so I happily walked down my real-life Monopoly board which two years earlier in India had seemed such a dream.

In the sun-baked courtyards we played, my two cousins and their friends, tossing our dice, collecting our rents, and making tidy piles of our paper money.

'I've been there!' stated an older cousin as he stopped to watch our wrangles over our shoulders. We froze and looked up at him in total amazement.

'Gosh, Ravibhai! Have you really?'

Ravibhai laughed at our delight as he squatted beside us followed by ten entranced eyes. We broke the short silence, simultaneously pushing forward our property cards.

'Ravibhai! Ravibhai! Have you been here? And Ravibhai, Ravibhai! Have you been there? Coventry Street, Regent Street, Park Lane? Waterworks?'

He nodded or shook his head and tossed the laughter about. The courtyard resonated with childlike enchantment as we changed the rules and adopted new values. Who cared now about Mayfair unless Ravibhai had been there!

'I won't charge you for landing at Paddington, Meera, 'cause that's where Ravibhai took his train to Oxford!'

The Monopoly board had exuded a new magic.

But Piccadilly was safe, quite safe. Safe from jail, safe because Ravibhai had been there, and now I was there and felt safe. Oh yes, Piccadilly was safe, quite safe.

A plane too was always safe. Whichever way I was going, I was always on my way home. From my first journey at the age of five and the countless ones in between, I have always been on my way. One day I will surely get there! This morning I awoke at home in London, tomorrow I will awaken at home in Delhi . . . and for now, I can sleep, safely, in my space; my home in the clouds . . .

Two

The day always starts early. Just before the break of dawn is the most auspicious time, and the morning prayers and incantations of the early risers that break the stillness of the night soon merge and harmonise with the chirping crickets, the twittering birds, the barking dogs and the waking cows. By 6 a.m. all self-respecting people are awake.

The early morning dreams drift and weave themselves into the sounds of the waking day. Lying in bed it is difficult to imagine that this is a big city. The residential colonies of the capital are like little worlds in themselves. What is it that makes time so still here? What creates this strange feeling of encapsulation? How . . . I wonder?

'Raniji, raniji.' The little sweeper girl stands with her broom at the side of my bed. 'Raniji, shall I get you a bucket of water?'

With my reverie interrupted, momentary irritation crowds out my democratic sense.

'Why? What for?' I snap.

'For your bath, raniji.' The reply is cheekily hesitant. In return I give her a severe, searching look. She looks down and proceeds to rub her naked feet against each other vigorously.

'You want me to get up so you can clean the room. Is that it?' She smiles and rubs her feet with more energy.

'Ah, well,' I yawn. 'Is everyone up?'

'Oh yes, raniji, everyone is up, prayers and breakfast all finished, all finished.'

'Okay then. Get my water.'

'Oh yes, raniji. At once, raniji.' The child throws down the reed broom in a quick movement as she darts off.

'And then, you bring me my tea.'

She rears to an abrupt halt and turns back.

'What – me, raniji?' The button eyes dart back in astonishment.

'Yes, you, raniji, and only you, raniji.'

The childish face breaks into a beam of unabashed delight.

As I bathe I imagine the unvoiced murmurs: 'Oh dear! Oh dear! These Western ways! She sleeps until nine and then drinks tea from the hands of an untouchable. Oh dear!' Of course, no one will say anything and whatever incredulity there might be will be quietly contained in genuine courtesy. If I didn't know, no way could I know! The reflection made me smile.

As I dress and drink sips of tea, the little girl watches, squatting on the floor of the newly swept bedroom and in no hurry to finish off the bathroom.

'You know in England I sweep my own rooms.'

'Don't you have a sweeper?'

'No, I do it myself. But I do have a machine.'

'A machine?' Her arm gestures a large outline.

'It's not that big. Only a little machine. I do it twice a week.'

'And who does it the rest of the time?'

'No one.'

'No one?'

'No. There isn't as much dust there you see.'

She doesn't see. 'I sweep and wash the floors twice a day and each time there's so much dust, raniji. In summertime it's even worse, the dust is so thin . . . '

Dust in the summertime! 'Smaller even than the smallest particle of dust thrown up by a chariot wheel in summer!' These were the words used by the Buddha to describe the microscopic nature of the *kalapas*: the subatomic particles in continuous flux and motion that constitute all matter –

4

including human beings. A quintessence of dust!

I look at the little girl and smile as she smiles back at me.

'Aha, that reminds me. I've got something for you.' From my case I pull out a blonde baby doll.

The little girl gasps and holds her breath.

'Here. Take it. It used to be Maya's.'

She doesn't move. Her mouth wide open, she stares with disbelief.

'It's yours now,' I tell her as I place the doll on the floor beside her. She crouches back.

'You must look after it. Give it a name.'

Minoo looks at the doll and nods as her button·eyes dance again and her face bursts into a wide smile.

Three

The large drawing room of my great-aunt's house with its Indianised Victoriana reflects the affluence and lifestyle of a bygone era. In the armchair sits Bibiji, my great-aunt, writing industriously. At her feet squats Maie, her old maidservant. On the far side of the room, the twelve-seater dining table, laid for one, is being attended to by another silver-haired lady, my aunt.

My appearance sets in motion a flurry of activity.

'She's come!' my great-aunt informs my aunt, who is already moving towards me with outstretched arms.

'She's come!' my aunt tells the maie who has nearly reached the kitchen door.

'She's come!' The maie opens the squeaking kitchen door and informs the cook.

'Yes, she's come! She's come!' repeats my aunt, gathering me in her embrace. Simultaneously my great-aunt says, 'Come, baby, sit,' and the old maie says, 'I've told him,' and sits.

'Merijaan ageii, my life has come,' murmurs my aunt, 'but so thin!'

'Come on, Daya, she's not at all thin. Just tired. Let her sit down and see about her breakfast.'

'Yes, yes,' my aunt quickly pats my cheek as she hurries off to the kitchen. Bibiji, smiling, gives me a mischievous wink and indicates with a slight lift of her eyebrows that I sit.

My great-aunt fills the large wicker and wood armchair like a throne. From its strategic position she can survey all the exits and entrances: the hall, the veranda, the garden, the

6

entrance gate, and the whole room. Her grey-blue shawl flows down from her shoulders on to the folds of her pale blue silk sari. Her shimmering white hair, drawn into a bun, frames her face, enhancing the jet blackness of her long lashes and large eyes. Groomed and composed, she is poised for the day. The single tooth in her top jaw gleams mischievously. At eighty, she is still a fine, healthy, sturdy, and dignified lady.

Next to her is a tall, two-tiered table. Earlier, it held her breakfast and now, cleared, it holds her accessories for the day: her bag, address book, pens, and old diaries, like the one in her hand in which she is writing 'ram, ram, ram' in miniscule letters and will continue to do so throughout the day, covering the sides, the margins, the old appointments . . .

At about 11 a.m., when the sun moves into the front garden, so too will Bibiji and her table. Her daily durbar will then open, the audiences will begin, and the stream of visitors will start to flow: neighbours, friends, protegées . . .

This is the winter schedule, when the nights are long and the sun doesn't heat till mid-morning.

'Tomorrow you sit here and have your breakfast on a tray next to me.' Her mischievous tooth dances as she speaks. 'But for today, you'd better sit at the table your masi has prepared for you. She's been fussing all morning.'

The table looks like a celebration! Fruit, sweets, nuts, dried fruit, and a miscellany of jams, pickles, preserves, all tastefully arranged on a crisply starched, embroidered tablecloth.

'But, Masi! This is a feast!' I exclaim. My aunt smiles shyly and looks over her carefully arranged display before busying herself with straightening the toast rack and inspecting the silver milk jug.

'Sit down now and eat,' she says with playful impatience.

On my plate, in a miniature silver lotus, is a single puffed sugar sweet.

'That's prasaad, I saved it from my pilgrimage in the

summer. So you must now eat it.'

'How did you know when I would come?'

She smiles, picks up the sweet and hands it to me, murmuring under her breath as she does so, 'Ah ha, my devi! My rani! May God bless and keep you!' She watches to make sure that the sweet gets eaten. 'I didn't know whether you'd want an English breakfast or an Indian breakfast. There's everything. Eggs from Pushpa Masi's farm, jam from your Shanta Masi – '

'What did you have?' I interrupt.

'Who, me? Oh, I lead a simple life. I just had roti.'

'I'll have the same as you.'

'What? Just roti?' My aunt looks at me with a mixture of surprise and pleasure.

'She said she'll have the same as you, so she'll have roti, with butter, pickle and fresh cream.'

My aunt hides a little sheepish smile by busying herself once again. She removes the toast rack, egg cup and the other superfluities belonging to the English breakfast and quickly disappears through the squeaking door into the kitchen.

'Namaste, raniji.' Chandu the cook greets me with a smile as radiant as the sun, and without asking, proceeds to pour out my tea. 'I've made it weak like you like it.' He smiles. 'Is everyone at home well?'

'Everyone's well.'

He replaces the teapot on its stand and tells me that he will come and fill my next cup, that the pot is hot and I should not try to touch it. I laugh.

'You've come after a long time, Meera, rani.' He speaks as though paying me a compliment. A long time! It always feels so long getting here and once here as though I'd never left.

I sit at the table sipping my second cup of tea and drinking in my impressions and feelings. Behind me the swing door squeals as Chandu and Aunt Daya go in and out. To my left, grandfather fridge who presides in the dining area, grunts and snores, falters, and then, as though reminding himself

8

his duties are not yet over, splutters and settles back into a loud drone.

At my side my aunt tempts and tends . . . The old maie gives me a long toothless grin. It seems to me that she has been toothless since I can remember. And that old grandfather fridge has been snoring for ever. And that Bibiji has always reigned from the same armchair, placed so that her eyes are everywhere.

'You're not eating,' exclaims my aunt as she places a sweet on my plate.

'Sorry, Masi. But please, that's enough. Thank you, but no more. Please.'

'What is this "please, sorry, thank you" business?' Bibiji's deep masculine voice resonates through the room. 'You're not in England now. You're in India and there's no need for any "please, sorry, thank you" business here!' She is emphatic.

'But please, Aunty. No more, thank you.'

'Please, sorry, thank you! Did you hear, Aunty, there she goes again,' chirps my aunt.

'Okay then. But how do I say *no, enough*?'

'You don't. You eat,' replies my aunt simply. 'You're too thin,' she adds with definite petulance. I concede with a laugh and having agreed that it will be the last sweet, start to nibble at it.

'Shabash! Well done!' she says as she runs her hands down along the length of my hair. 'You've kept your nice hair long,' she says approvingly as she sits down beside me. Quiet for the first time she watches the slow disappearance of the sweet as she looks at me with infinite pathos, probably struggling with imagined images of my life. I smile.

'God bless you, my rani,' she bursts out. 'God keep you, my devi. Such a lovely, loving child you were . . . ' Her eyes brim with tears and unable to contain them, she rushes out of the room.

'Bas, bas! Enough! Let the child eat.' Bibiji's deep voice soothes.

9

Outside, the deep pink bougainvillaeas are ablaze as the sunlight streams through them into the garden. In the driveway Minoo, my little sweeper girl, now bathed and breakfasted, plays and waits to be sent on an errand . . .

At the appointed time and without further prompting, the kitchen door squeals, Chandu and his assistant appear, and along with the old maie go about the business of setting up Bibiji's new headquarters. From inside the house, the paraphernalia of table, telephone, books, papers, pens are all carried out, while simultaneously, outside, the gardener and Minoo move the cane chairs from the veranda and arrange them on the lawn. Bibiji, with the help of her cane, follows, issuing instructions along the way.

Bibiji's house is in a very respectable and recently established residential colony. Many such had sprung up to house, among others, the refugees from the Punjab following the Partition of India in 1947. The houses are owner-built, some owner-occupied and others rented out to diplomats and executives until the owners retire to take possession. The houses are arranged in circles and semi-circles around open parks. Bibiji's house is large with both a back and a front garden. The back garden, which opens out on to the park, is for the laundry, whereas the front garden which adjoins the internal colony road is for sitting in. And there, today, as on any other day during the cool season, Bibiji sits in her open durbar, next to her high table, filling up with 'ram, ram, ram' the pages of one of her old diaries. Behind her the sun glistens her hair to silver and a cascade of luminous deep pink bougainvillaeas frames her presence. Soon the five or six cane chairs will be filled by the first visitors . . .

'Rani, rani.' My aunt Daya rushes in, a lilt of excitement in her voice. 'Your Pushpa masi's on the phone . . . she says . . . ' My aunt tries to catch her breath. 'She wants to know if you'd like to visit her farm tomorrow morning. I can then come too.'

10

I nod my assent. 'Your Pushpa masi will come very early, but don't worry, I'll wake you and bring you tea.' My aunt speaks hurriedly as though our departure were imminent.

On the veranda, Minoo plays with her doll. 'Her name is Parvati,' she tells me as I come by.

'Hmmm, Parvati!' I sound impressed.

'She's my favourite devi.' The little girl smiles shyly and looks at her feet.

I stroll over to be the first visitor at Bibiji's durbar.

'Come, baby, sit, sit,' she greets me as I join her, interrupting her writing to give me a smile and watch me settle into the cane chair which crackles as it receives me. 'You must rest after your journey.'

'Just being here is a rest.'

'I know,' she replies with empathy and waits to see if I will say more. She resumes her writing, throwing me occasional glances and pretending she isn't and I likewise pretend that I don't see. Nothing will be asked, yet everything will be 'known' and clearly understood or misunderstood.

'You remember your cousin Deepa?' Bibiji writes as she speaks. 'Well she's just got married again. She's gone to live in Bombay with her son and husband. Times are changing! Nowadays,' she adds carefully, 'there is no longer any stigma attached to a divorced woman.' She continues writing. I look at her and wonder if I need reply to the remark. As though reading my thoughts she dispels the need. 'I don't know what suddenly made me think of Deepa. It must be because she used to ring me . . . ' She doesn't finish, as though aware how unconvincing she sounds.

'*Taze tazey mattar wallah* . . . ' In the distance the vegetable seller sings out the freshness of his wares. Along with the visitors, the day will also be flavoured by the calls of the passing street sellers and entertainers: the vegetable man, the onion garlic man, the cloth merchant, maybe the monkey dance or snake charmer, the sweet-potato wallah, the odd holy and not so holy beggar will all make their appearance at some point during the day. To me it always feels the same; past and present merge, and memory feels obliterated in continuum . . .

'When the sweet potato man comes, we'll have some together. Okay, rani?' She winks at me and her mischievous tooth dances as we both smile to one another and I lean back in my chair to soak up the warmth of the winter sun and to wait for the sweet-potato man. It is all so soothing and comforting – and Bibiji's presence is like . . . like a solid rock in a turbulent sea. I turn my head to look at her, and our eyes meet.

'Meera . . .' She appears to be measuring her words. 'Now I don't know about your life in England, and I'm not trying to pry,' she hastens to add, 'but seeing you here, I can't help thinking how far away you are.'

She stops and puts away her writing and continues talking, her voice softer and deeper than seems possible. 'I want you to understand that, for as long as I'm alive, you always have a home with me for as long as you like, just as you would have had . . .'

'I know, Bibiji.'

'Good,' she replies and picks up her book once again to resume her writing. As she does so a car stops outside and the doors slam. I sigh.

'It's the Kapoors. You go inside, rani, if you don't want to meet people now. I'll tell them you're resting.'

'I'll do that. And also there is some writing I want to do.'

'You go, rani. Write your letters. And Meera,' she adds as I leave, 'I'll also tell the sweet-potato man to come back another time.' She winks at me.

Four

My dear friend,

This morning I woke up in India! It's wonderful to be here!
My sudden urge to come has actually materialised, and the
last three weeks of juggling to find the time, the seat on the
plane, the leave, seem far behind.

Martin drove down to fetch Maya and dropped me at
the airport. As it turned out, my concern about leaving her
was unwarranted. She fluttered around her father quite
happily – and didn't seem to mind in the least that she
wasn't coming with me. In fact, as I watched them walk
away together, it was I who felt the pang, the twinge of
betrayal! He even suggested I take this time fully for me,
like I'd said I needed to do, and not write unless I felt I
wanted to. 'We'll be okay,' he said, 'but just confirm your
return!' He was being gracious, yet I felt rejected. It's
absurd really!

Now I'm here, I'm grateful for this much-needed spell
on my own, and even through the jet-lag I'm aware of the
mixture of feelings – of memories and emotions that India
arouses in me – a sort of trepidation and wonder! As a
child on my visits back I used to feel . . . almost
overwhelmed that I should be connected to all this. I feel
the need to reconnect . . .

It doesn't seem like three years since my last visit and its
painful circumstances. But I have come to terms with all
that. Now, I need to find, understand, something else – for

myself. I'm sure I did the right thing to come.

I'm staying with Bibiji, the great matriarch of the family, who never married – nobody knows why and nobody will ever find out, as no one will ask! She's always been more like my grandmother really, and now as the only surviving member of her generation, she's the grandmother to the whole brood of great nephews and nieces. But although she's the oldest, she's not the head of the clan, as that can only be a man – the next one down the line is some twenty years her junior!

It's also quite funny the way no one asks any direct questions and assumes the worst. Because I have come on my own with such short notice, they have concluded that something is wrong, and it must be the marriage and so there are the sympathetic looks, the eloquent silences, and the asides about divorce no longer having a stigma. Bibiji said that earlier today, and within the Indian context it was a supportive and generous remark! I let it pass, for what could I reply, since I myself feel as though I don't know what, or if, anything is wrong or not wrong. The only thing I know is that I am so happy to be here – and I'd like to leave my questions and uncertainties behind, along with the tick tock of the clock . . .

Five

I sit in the back seat of the car, half-asleep, half-awake . . . The highway to the city is busy with traffic. We lumber along in the slow lane, the car rattling as though ready to collapse under the weight of the loud, argumentative gossip of its occupants.

'A divorced woman with two children! It's absurd! The boy can't be allowed to ruin his life.'

'But if he says he loves the girl?'

'Huh, she's not a girl, she's a woman with two children. And in any case, Daya, what do you know? Have you now become an expert on love?'

Aunt Daya is silent. Older sisters may only be contradicted with deference and in this instance a suitable reply calls for reflection.

'Love, indeed!' continues Aunt Pushpa. 'What about his love for us? What sort of impression will it create? We'll become a laughing stock. The child doesn't understand.'

The car turns into a narrow lane, blowing up a cloud of dust.

'At thirty-three, you could hardly call him a child.' Aunt Daya is meek.

Aunt Pushpa in reply presses down on the accelerator. The road bends and as we screech round it revealed before us is a cow sitting comfortably blocking our path.

'Look out, sister!' cries Aunt Daya.

'I can see! I can see!' snaps Aunt Pushpa as she honks loudly and comes to a halt. The cow stays in its place, nonplussed but unperturbed.

'Hut, hut hut!' she calls, and honks some more, but the cow does not move.

Aunt Daya leans out of the other window and claps her hands smartly. They wait for a little while, then Aunt Pushpa starts the car. Slowly and threateningly she proceeds to drive towards the cow.

'Sister, sister, what are you doing?' exclaims Aunt Daya.

'You'll see. Now it will get up and move,' replies Aunt Pushpa with assurance, clamping down on the horn at the same time.

The cow looks at the driver and then simply turns away. Aunt Pushpa stops short in front of the cow and, leaving the engine on, shouts. But the cow hears nothing. She turns the engine off so that it will hear better, and swears! But the cow just doesn't appear to understand.

Pushpa jumps out of the car and strides towards the cow. She pats it to get it to rise and then tries to push it towards the pavement. Unsuccessful, she stands up in annoyance.

On the back seat is a box of fresh vegetables collected during the early-morning visit to the farm – the purpose of this journey. Aunt Daya calmly and efficiently tears off a handful of carrot greens which she hands out of the window to Aunt Pushpa. Pushpa takes the greens with resignation, throws them on the pavement and returns to the driving seat. Sitting down with a definite sigh of exasperation, she waits for the cow to move. The cow sits still. Pushpa hoots.

'No, sister, don't do that, wait,' says Aunt Daya with ever-growing efficiency, and taking a bunch of fresh, succulent spinach, she gets out of the car. Holding the bunch in one hand and a single leaf in the other she approaches the cow and offers the leaf.

'Come, come my lotus-eyed beauty. This is for you. Come now and eat it.' The cow looks placidly at my aunt, who attempts a reassuring smile.

'Are you going to feed all our lunch to the wretch?' calls out Aunt Pushpa.

'Quiet, sister, do you want to be here all day?' returns Aunty Daya. The cow accepts the leaf. 'Good, good, take, take,' soothes Aunt Daya as she slowly moves back towards the pavement, holding up the bunch of spinach temptingly. 'Come, my life. Come, my love, all for you, come, come,' she continues.

The cow concedes. Slowly, and with great dignity, she rises, and then ambles leisurely to the pavement. She accepts the spinach graciously and then goes and sits down comfortably near the greens.

We drive off. Within a gear change the discussion is resumed as though it had never been interrupted.

'Sleep, sleep, my queen.' Aunt Daya wakes me when we arrive. 'Rest in your room until lunchtime.'

Chandu the cook carries in the vegetables while I follow, and my two aunts join Bibiji, who has just taken up her position in the garden.

I stop in the empty drawing room. The little mouse I have disturbed scrambles out into the garden. Grandfather fridge wakes up with a groan. I look around at the familiar mixture of India and Victoriana: the thick, faded, tasseled drapes, heavy wicker and rosewood furniture, old photographs, portraits and the miscellany of gods and goddesses, cut glass and nick-nacks that adorn and clutter around. Through the open garden doors a sharp patch of sunlight obliterates half the dining area, the dust dancing in its shaft. As I turn to leave I overhear: 'Has she said anything?' Aunt Pushpa's voice is urgent.

'About what?' replies Bibiji with calculated calm.

'Her marriage, of course,' replies Aunt Pushpa, as though stating the obvious. 'What is she up to? I heard from someone that they've got separate homes now!'

'I don't know what you've been hearing or why you've been listening,' interrupts Bibiji in an emphatic tone of voice. The intended silence is achieved and she resumes: 'She's one of our girls. If anybody talks, you should stop

17

them. Whatever we know must come from her. What she tells us. If she tells nothing, we know nothing.' My 80-year-old great-aunt reprimands my 75-year-old aunt with the full authority of an elder.

'Yes, yes, Aunty, you're quite right. No, no, we've heard nothing.' My aunt is suitably chastened.

18

Six

My aunt Daya brings me my morning tea in spite of
Bibiji the elder's instructions that I should be allowed to
sleep. My aunt insists that I can still sleep and drink my tea
and go back to sleep or wake up. It provides me with a choice
and her with the opportunity of showering me with loving
care.

My bedside table is cluttered with little parcels – presents I
have been wrapping up the night before. She clears them
away quickly, puts down my tea and strokes my hair as
though I were a small child. To her, at seventy, I still am: I'm
only half her age and one of her own children. My aunt, who
was widowed young, never had children of her own; instead
she lavished her affection on any of her many nephews and
nieces who would accept it. In her eyes I deserve an extra
dose. She leaves my tea and goes out in her characteristically
hurried manner.

The sounds, the smells of the household's morning routine
drift around me: baths, massage, prayers, incense. When the
smell of sandalwood starts to waft into my room, I will know
it's 8 a.m. and Bibiji is at her prayers. Once these are over
she will move into the drawing room, occupy her great
armchair and permit the drama of the day to unfold.

But for now it is still early and outside the darkness still
lingers. A little moth flutters around the naked light bulb. I
resolutely make a bid to wake up; three weeks in India is too
short a time and there is much I need to do and understand. I
sip my tea and plan my day in my head: I will make

telephone calls, appointments, write letters, and post a parcel entrusted to me . . . sit in the sun . . . My room is strewn with wrapped and half-wrapped gifts. Nearly new, warm clothes for the servants, carefully selected and gleaned from jumble sales, now cleaned and packed, ready to be distributed and gratefully received. For family and friends, chocolates and spice packets. Wrapping up the little packets of cinnamon and cloves and nutmeg, I had reflected on the irony of bringing back spices to the East from the West – the reversal of the spice trade! For my aunt Daya I have brought a pair of warm tights and a flowered toilet bag. I add a spice packet and wrap it up – just in time.

'Ram ram, rani, ram ram.' Aunt Daya comes in hurriedly with some sandalwood paste, with which she anoints my forehead, and a few segments of orange, which she puts to my lips, saying: 'Here, eat this, eat this. It is prasaad from my puja, eat it with my blessings. Ram ram, rani, ram ram. God keep you, ram ram. God protect you. Be happy, be happy.' Having fed me the orange she sits down on my bed and looks around at the parcels. I hand her hers. She protests.

'No, no, no, no. You shouldn't bring presents for me. I don't need anything. I lead a very simple life with few needs in retreat from the world.'

'Please take it, Masi, it's my joy!'

'Aah, hah. You always were a warm-hearted girl. But you shouldn't spend your money on presents. For the servants it's all right, but not for the family. They all have so much already – too much. In a poor country like ours, so full of poor people, they have much more than they need.' She continues with slight indignation, 'I know. Like you I have also worked for my living and there is no need to spend money on people who have enough. I live a simple life. Now I'm retired I have a small place up in the hills near the banks of the mother Ganga. Yes, and Gangaji is like a mother, very soothing and beautiful. And every morning I go down to the river, take my bath and say my prayers – ' She interrupts herself, almost as though she is surprised that no one else has done so. 'Do you want to have your bath now? Shall I call Minoo to bring you your bucket of water?'

'No, no, Masi. I'll wait a little while.'

'Yes, of course, take your time and have a rest. The water will stay hot. Of course, I always bathe in cold water. Up in the hills the waters of the Gangaji can be very cold, but I still bathe there every morning. Then I say my prayers and greet the rising sun . . . ' She brings together the palms of her hands, briefly touching them to her forehead. '*Om bhur bhava swaha, tat savitur varenyam.*' She chants the Gayri softly. The five-thousand-year-old Vedic hymn resonates through my bones like an old echo. I am awed at its antiquity and continuity . . . My aunt is now silent, smiling, gazing, staring trance-like into an image she has evoked in her mind's eye.

'Every day after I have bathed and prayed, I thank God for everything and especially for the two great gifts I have received.' She looks at me. 'Do you know what two gifts I always thank the great Divine Being for?'

'No, Masi,' I tease, shaking my head, 'but I'm sure you're going to tell me.'

'Oh yes, I'll tell you. I'll tell you. The first great gift I thank God for is enabling me to lead an independent life. That, in spite of having no husband, I was able to earn my living and did not have to be dependent on anyone. That, rani, is a great thing. In India life can be very cruel for a woman on her own. I know. I've worked with destitute women all my life, widows and orphans and working girls, and it's very difficult. I've been very lucky. I had the support of my family. I got an education and work and now, even though I'm retired, I can live on my savings and pension and still be independent, and that, rani, is a great thing and every day I thank God for it.'

She savours her gratitude awhile before continuing: 'And the second thing I thank God for, every day, is that I was born in human form; that of all the creatures and forms of life I could have come as, I was able to come as a human being. Now that too, my rani, is a very great thing and I

21

thank God for it.' In response to my flickering smile she illustrates her point with seriousness.

'It's no laughing matter. After all, imagine, I could have come as a donkey, or a monkey, or some creepy-crawly – an insect.' She adds the last looking at the moth still hovering round the bulb, still slightly brighter than the outside light. She gets up to switch it off.

'What about a contented, carrot-eating cow!'

'Huttheri. Away with you!' She slaps my leg in mock indignation. 'You're making silly-style jokes now! Young people today think themselves too modern to understand some things. But you're a good girl,' she adds as she leans over to pinch my cheek and then, picking up the parcel, she bustles out of the room.

Seven

Bibiji's durbar has opened early and the drawing room is filled with neighbours and protegées, all silver-haired ladies, huddled in shawls, participating in an animated discussion and talking simultaneously. There must be a resoluteness in my step or a mark of determination in my face, for Bibiji, instead of inviting me as usual to 'Sit, sit . . .' by way of greeting, asks me instead where I'm going.

'To the post office. I have to send off a parcel.'

'You don't need to go to the post office yourself. I can send someone for you.'

'It's just that it's a friend's parcel . . . to be sent to West Bengal.'

'What's this? What's this? A parcel? Where to?' breaks in a neighbour.

'What? Where to?' asks another.

'She's got a parcel to send.'

'What, Meera, you've got a parcel? A parcel of what?'

'It's a parcel of clothes. To be sent to West Bengal.'

'Acchaa,' nods the first neighbour with an expression of understanding and then, turning to the others, says: 'She must be sending clothes to her cousin Renu in Calcutta.' An older cousin I hardly know and last met some fifteen years ago! But the logic is generally accepted and before there is time to clarify, the conversation has moved on to a discussion about Renu and the quality of life in Calcutta.

I pull up a cane stool next to Bibiji and look over her shoulder as she meticulously writes 'ram, ram, ram' over 'Welfare Board Meeting' in a 1960 diary.

'It's always best to send parcels through someone – and there are people going to Calcutta every day. Otherwise it has to be registered and what not. Once I remember Kishore had to bring a parcel back three times from the post office before they would accept it.'

'But it's not going to Cal, Bibiji. It's a friend's parcel – he's packed it and asked me to send it insured.'

'Okay, rani. Bring it here. But registering parcels is always a bother.'

The last comment is overheard by one of the ladies who exclaims as I leave the room: 'Registered. Oh no. Even registered parcels don't always reach . . . '

My return with a neatly wrapped and tied brown-paper parcel slowly silences the enthusiastic discussion on the pitfalls and problems of registration and insurance. The assembly look at me slightly dumbfounded and the silence makes Bibiji look up from her writing.

'Is that . . . ' starts a neighbour in a gentle tone, while the others around look ready to say something.

'Of course not,' leaps in my great-aunt. 'That's not the parcel, just the packet. I asked her to bring it to me to see the size.'

The assembly still looks unsure. Bibiji's look warns me to say nothing and I hide my bewilderment as the 'packet' is taken from my hands and given to Maie, who walks out of the room with it appearing to know exactly what she's doing.

'Bas. Hun hogayaa. It's done,' says Bibiji. Everyone understands that the parcel topic is closed and she resumes her writing by way of punctuation to any further discussion.

'In India parcels have to be wrapped in cloth,' she explains later when we are alone.

'I'd forgotten.'

'It doesn't matter, rani, but we don't want outside people imagining you're a tourist or something.'

'But I am – in a way.'

'Don't be silly. You're in your country, and we are your family '

24

The new parcel has been lined with polythene and tightly sewn into a raw cotton cover. The combined effort of Maie and Aunt Daya, it is inspected and admired. I am told it will have to be sealed with wax and stamped but nobody quite knows how. Aunt Daya can't remember having sent one and Bibiji entrusted such errands to Ashok, the bright son of one of her destitute protegées for whom she had found employment as a clerk some ten years ago, and who still came by every Friday to mark his eternal gratitude and perform any odd jobs.

'Pushpa bhenji will be coming soon,' remembers Aunt Daya. It is agreed that she will know exactly what to do, that it's the 'best idea' and we will wait . . .

By lunchtime Aunt Pushpa has still not come and I am dismayed. Time, which felt so comfortably suspended yesterday, now begins to feel irritatingly slow as I sense my well-planned day slipping by.

'She'll come, she'll come,' soothes Aunt Daya. 'If not by lunch, then at tea; if not tea, then after tea, but she'll come.'

Or the day after tomorrow or in a week, I feel like snapping. My aunt smiles and sure enough Aunt Pushpa's car grumbles into the driveway.

'See, rani,' beams Aunt Daya, going off to meet her sister.

'Bibiji, why don't I just take the parcel to the post office . . . instead of – '

'No, no, it's no bother. Your Pushpa masi will send it to your Ravibhai's office and he's got peons and clerks and PAs who'll get it done in no time. We'll ask her you'll see.'

Aunt Pushpa will get it done. 'Nothing to it,' she declares, placing the parcel beside her. The ever-energetic widow of a senior civil servant and used to exercising authority, she is always pleased when her resourcefulness and expertise are called upon. Though a 'Bibiji', 'Burri mem sahib', and 'Mataji' in her own right, with her own satellites of dependents and protegées, she is particularly pleased when her resourcefulness is recognised by her own paternal aunt, Bibiji. She pulls out her knitting, another area of expertise

25

which she performs quite effortlessly, producing the most intricate patterns. Her hands not only appear to work quite independently, but also seem to free and activate her mind. The jersey, she informs us, is for the grandson of a VIP, a special request from the boy himself. Last week she finished half a dozen socks for a grandson at Yale and after the jersey she is going to make half a dozen for her eldest son. Since her last visit, three days ago, she has helped Madan with his transfer, Mrs Kapur to get compensation for a land acquisition, which involved a visit to the courts in Old Delhi, a widowed neighbour to sort out her estate duties, visited two sick people in hospital, been asked to find a girl for the Chopra boy, and on her way back is to have tea with Kanta, who wants advice on her forthcoming marriage. The socks were finished just in time to hand to Shiv, who was flying that same evening to New York and had promised to buy some special wool during his stopover in London on his way back.

Aunt Daya listens, enthusiastically nodding with pride at her sister's prowess. Bibiji's hand appears to have tightened over her pen as her writing gets more measured. She glances at her nieces without raising her head.

'Don't worry at all about your parcel, darling.' Aunt Pushpa smiles, having interrupted her narrative to tie a new ball of wool on to her knitting. 'I'll have it sent through Ravi's office as soon as he gets back from Cairo in three days.'

'Three days!' I bolt up. 'Why don't I just take it myself to the post office this afternoon?'

My irritation bursts out and I am taken aback by the ungraciousness of my tone. My aunts start, and then speak simultaneously: 'But, no, no, no.' 'But, why, why, why . . . let your Pushpa masi do it. Let Ravi's office do it. The post office will take you half a day. Or even the whole day. You won't be able to do it. You won't be able to get the right information. Not even your parcel – your holiday. What's the hurry anyway . . .'

I recognise that there isn't any hurry except that the day is not unfolding as programmed! 'It's just that . . . I thought I'd get it out of the way. Take it to the post office myself and . . . and . . . learn . . . what to do.'

The last is tentatively said and no sooner spoken than I wish I could swallow it back. 'Huh! What learn! You're going to be sending parcels every day now that you want to learn?' Aunt Pushpa mocks, then, lilting her voice to affect resignation and endurance, adds: 'If there's such a hurry, I'll take it now . . . I'll call up Kanta and go and see her later.'

This time it is both Aunt Daya and I who are about to speak simultaneously but we are silenced by Bibiji's baritone: 'No, no, Pushpa. No need to call Kanta. Let Meera take the parcel herself.'

Startled, I look at Bibiji just in time to catch the sparkle of triumph in her eyes and the mischievous gleam of her single tooth before she quickly resumes her expression of demure detachment. 'It's good,' she adds, 'that the child wants to learn . . . ' The grip on her pen has loosened and the writing flows. 'Why don't you just drop her at the post office on your way back?'

'Meera!' She calls me back while my two aunts walk towards the car. Her eyes are sparkling again. 'Don't worry too much about the parcel.' The mischievous tooth gives her strategy away. 'If you don't post it, I'll send for Ashok tonight and he will send it off tomorrow morning. First thing!' She resumes writing.

27

Eight

The post office is a noisy bustle. Different counters dealing with different transactions, but none specifically for parcels.

'You'll just waste three hours!' was my aunt's parting remark and I begin to see what she means. I stand in the queue and observe that some don't – they simply march up alongside the queue and carry out their business over the counter grilles. As I wonder about trying this tactic myself, our queue is summarily dismissed to another, and the counter closed. 'Ah well, one can but try!' I say to myself and make my way up to the closed counter and address the clerk who appears to be logging receipts.

'Bhai sahib, namaste. Please could you help me?' I start. 'I have a difficulty for which I need your advice.' He glances at me and I quickly add, 'I'll just wait here till you have a moment.' He continues his work and after a short while raises his head, looks at me, gives his head an upward nod, a movement which means, 'Well what is it?'

I show him the parcel, quickly explaining that it has to be insured, that I've never sent one before and need to know exactly what to do.

His reply is transmitted through two economical gestures: a slow lowering of the eyelids to say he's understood, a glance at the parcel and simultaneously a quick lift of the eyebrows to signify that I should hand it to him.

He looks it over and then speaks to me for the first time in a tone of benevolent paternalism. 'Now sister, understand me well by listening to me carefully,' he starts. 'You see this stitching?' He runs his fingers along Aunt Daya's handiwork. 'Now all along this stitching, this much apart' – it looks like three inches – 'you must seal it. You must put hot wax and stamp it with a seal. That's what you must do. Do you understand?'

'Yes, yes,' I reply and put my hands out to retrieve the parcel.

'Now understand this!' he continues. 'It is important that the mark of the seal must not be broken. If it is broken, then I cannot take the parcel.'

'Yes, yes, I understand.'

He looks at me to make sure that I do and slowly hands me back the parcel. 'When you've sealed it properly bring it back to me and I'll send it off. You'll find what you need in the market opposite,' he adds as though anticipating my question.

The wax is easily obtained, but the seal! Seals, I am told, cannot just be bought. They have to be made, created; they are personal items and not in stock as such. Of course they can be ordered . . . would take only a few weeks . . . or maybe just a few days. Another shop? Maybe . . . could try and see?

Another shop . . . and another . . . and another, but none sell seals! I am told I could probably get one in Connaught Circus or in Old Delhi, and though no one seems to know exactly where, all assure me that I'll have no trouble finding out – once I'm there!

The last shop in the row is a bookseller who, like them all, shakes his head at my request. It is an English bookshop, quiet and surprisingly uncrowded. Reminding myself that I had planned to visit a bookshop during my stay, I start to browse, but I am unable to lift my attention from the weight of the packet in my bag . . . I look around vacantly . . .

'What sort of a seal are you looking for?' The voice comes from an inner office hidden behind the bookshelves and merging in with the book-covered walls. At a desk sits an

29

older man in a maroon turban, also blending in with the books and the shelves. I find myself rushing towards him, sitting down unasked, pulling out the parcel and spilling out my story in flustered frustration.

'Here!' he replies with a smile, opening his desk drawer. 'Use my seal.' He leans over and hands it to me.

I stare at it. A simple brass oval shape with a monogrammed G.B.S. Nothing at all spectacular – but for me, at this moment, it is like . . . like . . .

'It's wonderful!' I blurt out, and then correcting myself, 'I mean it's such a wonderful relief! I'd almost given up hope!'

'Aha. You must never ever give up hope. This is nothing. It is my privilege to be of help – and if you'd told any other shop that you just needed to use a seal, they would have lent you theirs if they had one.'

'I didn't think of that,' I reply.

'You have one now! And you can seal your parcel here. Don't get up, stay sitting, and I'll call for some tea.' As he speaks he clears a space on his desk and out of the. drawer pulls out a stick of red sealing-wax and matches. He disappears through a little opening hidden among the books, calls out for the tea and returns with a tumbler of water which he places in front of me. I take a sip out of politeness. He watches, smiles and nods his head.

'Shall I have the parcel sealed for you?'

'No, no,' I reply. 'Please don't trouble. I'll manage! The man in the post office told me what to do.'

Confidently, I light a match, melt the wax on to the parcel and crush the seal on. As I lift it, half the wax comes off on the seal leaving behind an unsightly smudge and only half a G. The old man smiles as though he expected this and says kindly, 'You have never done this before. My assistant will do it for you when he brings the tea.'

I drink my tea and watch the assistant as he deftly makes a circle of red wax, dips the seal into the tumbler of water, presses it down, lifts it, leaving behind a perfectly formed, crisp indentation. Moving down the seams one after the other, each stamp is perfectly embossed.

'The water prevents the wax from sticking to the seal.'

'I'm lucky I came here. I'd never have known what to do otherwise.'

'No, no,' he replies. 'Someone else would have helped you. It was just my privilege to do so.'

He hands me the sealed parcel looking like a cherry cake.

'Sardarji, thank you so much for your kindness . . . '

'Nothing at all, my child, nothing at all . . . God keep you.'

Packed, sealed, stamped, insured, to my relief the parcel is off. I look at my watch and note that my adventure has taken me less than an hour!

As I return home the transition from the day to the evening is starting. Taxis and autorickshaws no longer beckon, but wait – for a fare that will take them home. The cows, who in the morning had been let loose on the charity of the bazaars, now amble homewards to rest after the day's pilfering, strutting along the roads with the same confident right of way as the two-, three- and four-wheelers. The bus queues burst and spill into the road. The birds descend on their nests in a loud squawking, quarrelling, cooing and crooing . . . and everywhere people prepare and wait to return – as others prepare and wait to welcome them. Soon it will be dark. The change will be abrupt; a final burst of colour, of sound, of light. A short flash of twilight and the blanket of dark will envelop the city.

As my autorickshaw clangs into the quiet colony road, twilight has not yet flashed. The dhobi's five-year-old son runs in and out of the houses delivering the day's ironing. In the meantime, his mother packs up the ironing cart, while his father warms his hands on the drying embers as he waits for the irons to cool.

On the veranda sits Bibiji, transforming the creaky chair into a throne. Her grey-blue shawl draped over her shoulders, cane in hand, she is ready for her evening stroll to inspect and ensure the peaceful transition of the day into the evening. As I walk up the drive, her eyes dance and her tooth twinkles.

'Come,' she invites. I hand my bags to Minoo and walk out alongside my great-aunt, slowing my steps to match hers.

'So!' she starts. 'You've posted that parcel?'

'Yes.'

'Very good, very good. And you found out what to do?'

'A man in a shop did most of it for me.'

'Acchaa! . . . That's very good! Which shop was it?'

'A bookshop at the end of Khan Market,' I reply, wondering what difference it makes.

At this time the roads of the colony become a strolling ground for pedestrians before the cars returning from the city come rumbling in, raising dust . . .

'What was his name?'

'Who?'

'The shop in Khan Market. The man's name?'

'Oh him! Gurbachan Singh.'

'A young man or an old man?'

'About sixtyish,' I reply, again wondering why on earth she should want to know the name of a shopkeeper in a market miles away.

'Hmm, Gurbachan Singh! I would need to know his father's name . . . Usually if they are from Lahore I can recognise the names. Lahore people are very helpful. When you meet them tell them you're from Lahore. Our families were very well known there.'

Bibiji's remark silences out the world as another sound swells: Lahore! I silently sound the word in my head and plummet into the mythical meanings of the city of my origins and ancestors. Lahore, now in Pakistan – from which I was uprooted at the age of three, and somewhere along the way lost . . . Me . . . from Lahore? 'The old days in Old Lahore . . . ' is how the stories used to begin . . .

'You were much too little to remember, but I used to take you for walks in the Lawrence Gardens and tonga rides along the Mall Road and you used to chatter away . . . '

32

We stroll along, each in our memories and meanings. Bibiji stops to exchange greetings along the way. I follow, imitate, smile, nod, fold my hands to namaste – while my mind strays . . . reaching out?

'Meera? Meera!'

'Yes, Bibiji.'

'You're in dreamland!'

'Yes! It all seems so far away . . . Lahore . . . '

'Ah yes! So much ended with the Partition! You were too young to remember . . . and then you all went so, so far away . . . ' She shakes her head. 'Come, let's go back,' she says and leans on my shoulder. 'Tell me if there's too much weight.'

'No there isn't. I like it. It's comforting.'

Lying in bed the sound swirls in my head. Lahore . . . Lahore . . . As though the repetition would unlock the mystery and free my thoughts from being stuck in the tortuous conditional: if . . . What would I be and what my life if, if and if . . . And now? Could I return? What would it mean? What would I need to know? Who to ask? What questions?

Outside a car rumbles in, breaking the night silence. Gates clang, doors slam. No doubt residents returning from a dinner party. Then, once again, all is quiet, the streets empty, except for the stray dogs who remain, and complain, that they have nowhere to return to . . .

But tomorrow I can find out –

Obtain the information – find my questions.

Explore the possibilities – and who knows what they might be.

Nine

My watch has stopped, but I know from the sounds it is morning. I love the sounds: the mixture, the medley, the richness, the perspective. The pattern and panorama of life. I lie still – as absolutely still as I possibly can – to listen – and hold my breath to try and catch the most distant sounds – only to lose them in Maie's shrill reply to Bibiji's drone of a baritone next door.

Yes indeed I love the sounds. They are comforting and reassuring and have so completely dispelled the night's tossing, the tortuous conditionals, clearing the way to a new day. Yes, a new day in which I can feel free to imagine, at least, just how very nice it would be to wake up to the sounds of India every morning. But why only imagine? Last night I went to sleep with the resolve that I would find out and explore possibilities . . . I shall start with Bibiji. Join her in her room for tea . . .

Bibiji has just finished her morning massage and is sitting by the one-bar electric fire reading the morning newspaper and drinking a cup of tea – set out on her ever-faithful two-tiered table. At her feet Maie closes up the jars of massage cream and rubs the residue from her hands on to her own arms and legs. As I enter she asks me with a toothless grin, a chuckle laugh, and a clap of the hands if I too want a massage. I shake my head.

'Tomorrow,' she replies in an intonation which is both a question and a statement.

34

'Tomorrow,' I repeat with the same ambiguity, and laugh as I realise the ambiguity of the word itself – in Hindi the same word is used to mean both tomorrow and yesterday!

Chandu calls at the door. Maie is instructed to bring in my tea as Bibiji folds away her newspaper and turns to me.

'Come, baby, sit by the fire. Pull the chair up. So, you slept well?'

'No. But I woke up well.'

'Acchaa. That's the main thing. But tell me.'

'I think it was just all this talk of Old Lahore yesterday.' Bibiji nods her head in empathy. 'It just sort of . . . brought a lot of stuff to the surface . . . '

'Stuff? To the surface? What does that mean?'

'It means becoming aware of things that one was not conscious of . . . or didn't fully realise.'

'Acchaa. I see . . . ' Bibiji waits for me to continue.

'I was thinking I'd like to explore a bit and find out if and how I could maybe come back and live here – for a long spell at least – if such a thing would be at all possible . . . '

Bibiji nods thoughtfully as though weighing her words and searching for the appropriate thing to reply. 'Everything is possible . . . '

'Shall I get the flowers?' interrupts Maie.

Bibiji is visibly disturbed. 'Maie!' she exclaims in a deliberate tone meant to express her exasperation. 'Tell me, Maie, how long have you been with me? Thirty years? More? And don't you go out every day and pick the flowers while I have my tea? Do you or don't you?'

'Sometimes I don't go until you're in the bath.'

'Ohhh! Whatever and whichever time! But every day you go out and pick the flowers. Why then must you ask me if you must pick the flowers and interrupt when you can see that I am talking?'

'I'll go and get the flowers then,' replies Maie, mumbling under her breath as she leaves the room, loud enough so that she can be heard, 'When you ask they say why do you ask, when you don't ask they say why do you not ask, when you

just go off and do something they say who told you to go off
. . . Whatever you do it's never right.' She smiles at me as
she leaves the room and I start to laugh at the familiar
interaction. Bibiji, however, is less amused and gathers up
her mala to re-establish her calm, muttering under her breath
as she does so.

'I've said to her, "Maie, you're old now, why don't you go
to your sons in the hills, I'll give you a pension," but no, she
has to stay here and argue! It's my karma!'

I laugh happily. 'You must be each other's karma.'

Bibiji fingers her mala and smiles at my laughter. 'Yes,
yes. What were we saying before . . . I've fogotten.'

'You said anything is possible . . .'

'Yes, yes. That's right. Anything is possible. Only *you* can
decide what's the right thing to do. There will be things you
need to work out from there, but there are things you can
find out from here. For that you must meet the family. Talk
to them, ask their advice. Even if your parents are no longer
here, the family is here. That's the way things are done in
India . . .'

That's the way things are done in India! I'm sure the
episode of the parcel is going through her mind.

'Also try to meet the younger generation – Usha, Sita –
and the older ones as well. Start with your uncle Kishore.'

'Okay. I'll do that today.'

Ten

My dear friend,

The word 'kal' is used to mean both yesterday and tomorrow. Maybe they *are* the same, in that neither of them is here and now – which is today. Today I will meet Uncle Kishore.

Everything about being here is intoxicating and this morning I awoke with a feeling, almost a yearning, that I'd like to stay – at least for a while; there is something I need to integrate and fit together again.

On the plane I looked around at all the people, and watched the patterns of my thoughts as I wondered who was visiting, who was returning and what I was doing. Possibly my rambling reflections and half-voiced questions were the surfacing of that need, which I must now explore. Could I . . . actually return? Yesterday the talk of Lahore awakened my whole feeling of uprootedness and loss – of my parents, city, home, country; the years of feeling suspended. I need to change that. My connection to India was through my parents, now I must make it myself.

It was thoughtful of Martin not to expect me to write. I wouldn't know what to say or how to share my thoughts. Could it be that our enforced separation of these past six months is a natural prelude . . . to something else . . . to my eventual return? Who knows! I need to get a sense of what life would be like, what I could do and how one gets things done. I'm still unclear about it all, but over the next few weeks I'm sure that some clarity will emerge. Dear Maya! I'll start by finding out about schools for you.

I'll see what Uncle Kishore has to say and start the day.

Eleven

'Hmm,' says my uncle thoughtfully, nodding his head. 'So. You want to "explore possibilities" and "obtain information". That's right?'

'Well, yes . . . ' I reply, wondering if there isn't a slight irony in his tone. I decide it's probably just hearing my own words and their vagueness.

'Yes, that's it,' I confirm.

'Well . . . of course there's no mystery about obtaining information in India. It's like anywhere else. You just have to be clear what you want to know, where to go, and who to ask.' To emphasise the simplicity of the matter, he slaps his hands on his knees, then raises them, palms uplifted, before bringing them once again down on his desk to lever himself up from his large swivel armchair – all done with the clear assurance of a man who knows his whats, wheres and whos.

'Go and see your uncle Kishore,' Bibiji had said to me in the morning. 'Go and talk to him. He will have some good ideas. He knows everything that's going on, and everybody. Of course, he's very busy, but if you go at lunchtime, you'll be able to see him. He always keeps lunchtime free for the family. He's a good boy.'

I watch my 60-year-old, grey-haired uncle as he paces up and down slowly.

'A good boy,' I laugh softly.

'So, what's so funny eh?'

'Nothing really,' I reply. 'It's just that Bibiji said you were a good boy.'

'Did she!' He hides his pleasure. 'Good boy, indeed! Hmm. Yes . . . in India, my dear child, they always want to keep you as children. Families do it to their kin, the government does it to the people . . . they all do it.' With the last remark he sinks into the sofa and in a tone which betrays a tinge of childlike grumpiness calls out to the office peon to bring in two coffees.

'Now to get back to you. You need to . . . get information, so that you can "explore possibilities".'

They were my own words, I remind myself. However, hearing them repeated they seem to echo the very vagueness of my questions, the uncertainty of my exploration. It would be nice if I could be a child and be told what I must do . . .

'Now what you must do,' my uncle addresses the ceiling fan, 'is to start off with some of the specific things you mentioned. Right?'

'Yes, right,' I reply confidently.

'So, what were they?' He looks at me. Fortunately, before I have time to remember what I've forgotten, he turns, returns his gaze to the fan and continues, 'Ah yes, you said your girl was keen on music and you'd like to know about good schools and centres. Right?'

'Right.'

'So. You make that your starting point. Delhi is the best place to find information. For this, all you need to do is go to the All-India Music Institute in Amrita Shergill Marg. You go there and ask them and they'll tell you.' He looks at me. 'You know the place?'

I look vague.

'You know Ratendon Road?'

I nod.

'Well, the old Ratendon Road is now Amrita Shergill Marg. I haven't got a driver this afternoon otherwise he could have taken you in the car. But any taxi or scooter rickshaw will take you there.' He gets up from the sofa and returns to the desk. 'I just remembered. Raghu Rajan has been appointed the new director and should have arrived

40

from Calcutta by now. You go straight to see him, straight to Raghu Rajan.'

'Shouldn't I call and make an appointment?'

'No, no, no. Delhi telephones are useless. You just go there on your way home and if he's not there fix an appointment on the spot. That's the best way.'

'Raghu Rajan,' I repeat. 'I'll just write the name down.'

'What, you don't know Raghu? Well never mind, he'll know you. Just say I sent you and who you are. Hukum!' He calls out to the office peon and intructs him to bring me a rickshaw. 'In any case he'll know who you are. Your father and he were good friends in Lahore.' Lahore again . . . always Lahore. 'Come and see me again and tell me how you get on. I'm sure Raghu will help.'

The rickshaw drives me right into the porch of an unmarked building.

'Is this it?'

'Yes, yes, this the place. Shall I wait?'

'No, it's not necessary,' I reply confidently as I pay.

The receptionist nods his head with assurance and directs me to the first floor, where I am directed in turn to the second floor. There they have never heard of Raghu Rajan and return me again to the first floor. My heels click noisily as I go down the marble stairs. I return to the office on the first floor – a long room with six desks jammed along one wall, shelves and cupboards on the other and a narrow passage in between. The clerk at the first desk nearest the door doesn't look particularly surprised to see me back.

'You sent me to the accounts department,' I say accusingly.

'Acchaa, they couldn't help you,' he replies with sympathy.

'They said the Music Institute was on this floor.'

'Yes, that's quite right. The Music Institute is here. Please wait one minute.' He gets up from his desk and manoeuvres his way to the end desk, the largest one in the room next to the only window. After exchanging a few words with its occupant, he beckons me across.

'This is the Music Institute, isn't it?' I start.

'Oh yes, madam,' confirms the occupant of the larger desk.

'I would like to see Raghu Rajan.'

He looks at me blankly.

'Raghu Rajan,' I insist. 'He's been appointed director here – in charge of the Music Institute.'

'Acchaa. Please wait one minute. Please sit, madam.' He points to a chair and then calls out towards the door. 'Call Krishna!' The message is relayed along: 'Call Krishna . . . call Krishna . . . call Krishna . . . ' 'Krishna's gone to the post office . . . ' the message is relayed back. 'Will you have some tea?' he asks rising. I shake my head.

'Then please you wait, madam. I will just come. Thank you,' he says squeezing his way past.

The five occupants of the other desks, three men and two women, glance at me as they work. The woman closest to where I am sitting smiles shyly. The smile I return feels a bit stiff.

'You won't have any tea?' she says.

'No. I just had something before coming.'

She nods. 'You've come from outside?'

'From outside? . . . Yes, yes I've come from outside.'

'From America?'

I shake my head but before there is any time to go any further a message is relayed down and our attention directed to the door where the man from the big desk stands signalling that I join him.

'I've come from England,' I tell her, getting up to go, and as I leave the room I hear the information relayed down, 'She's come from UK . . . from UK . . . UK . . . '

The corridor echoes the click of my heels. 'Thank you for your help,' I say above the sound.

'No mention, no mention,' he replies. 'I am taking you to Swami sahib. He will help you.'

I am led into another office, larger than the first, but with only three desks this time. Swami sahib greets me, invites me to sit while my escort leaves.

'I would like to see Raghu Rajan.'

He nods. 'Your good name please?'

'Meera. Meera Sahgal.' It is my maiden name that slips out.

'Rajan sahib is at present out of station. He will come back next week.'

'Next week!' I sound alarmed. 'It's just that I'm only here for a couple of weeks.'

'Well, if you come back next week, Rajan sahib will be here and you will be able to see him.'

'Yes, I understand. Maybe there is somebody else who could help me. You see I want to find out about music centres and schools . . . '

'Yes, yes. This is the All-India Music Institute.'

'Yes, I know. That's why . . . maybe there is someone else who could advise me . . . I mean do you have any information . . . any brochures?'

'Brosh– ?'

'Yes, you know, leaflets or . . . books . . . something which gives me information about music centre places.'

'This is the All-India Music Institute,' he repeats gently. 'We have all information here.'

'Do you have anything I can see?'

'Oh yes, we have everything. Rajan sahib will show you.'

'But don't you have any leaflets? Like in the tourist office you know, they have leaflets . . . about places to visit and . . . '

'Oh yes, yes.' He shakes his head with understanding. 'You may please try the tourist office for leaflets and Rajan sahib will be back next week.'

I sigh.

'Will you have some tea or water?' he asks kindly. I shake my head and rise to leave.

'Rajan sahib will be here next week,' he tells me again with a smile. 'You may please come next week.'

'Shall I make an appointment?'

'No, no need. You just please come next week.'

Outside in the street there is not a rickshaw in sight. From my crossroads point I wonder which direction to take, my choice eventually dictated by the position of the hot sun as I choose to walk away from its glare. My high heels sink into the dust on the pavement. I mentally note the unsuitability of my Western shoes – unless, of course, one travels by car. Tomorrow I will buy some chappals.

In the garden it is teatime. Bibiji sees me coming and calls out: 'Come, rani, come. Sit, sit. Have some tea. It's just been made.'

'Yes, yes. It's just been made,' confirms my aunt Daya. 'I'll make you somkk Sit.'

'Acchaa! So tell us.' Bibiji's deep voice soothes. 'How was your day?'

'I don't know. Okay I suppose.'

'Acchaa?'

'I felt a bit like that girl in the children's rhyme – you know the one who goes to the bazaar to buy an aloo and forgets it because she's chased by a bhaloo.'

'Aha ha, you remember that!' chips in Aunt Daya. 'And then she goes to buy some dhania and forgets it because she's chased by the bania. I used to sing it to you when you were little.' She hands me my tea and bursts into the song.

'Bas bas, Daya,' Bibiji interrupts. Aunt Daya continues the song humming to herself softly.

'Tell me then, rani. What sort of a . . . bhaloo?' enquires Bibiji.

'What? What? Was there a bhaloo in the city? You saw a bear? A dancing one – ' interrupts Aunt Daya.

'Daya,' Bibiji raises a severe tone, 'you don't listen. You always interrupt. Never let anyone finish.'

Aunt Daya looks puzzled and hurt. Her chin trembles slightly.

'The child was trying to say something.'

At the mention of the child Aunt Daya turns to me with a

quizzical look which soon transforms into a smile.

'And tomorrow? What are you going to do tomorrow?' asks Bibiji.

'Tomorrow,' I sigh, 'tomorrow I am going to buy some chappals.'

'Shabash,' says Aunt Daya, and claps her hands.

Twelve

I am waiting for a cousin who is meeting me for a quick lunch sandwiched between her busy executive's schedule. She is late.

The restaurant appears dark and sultry, the light blocked out by the heavy air conditioners and smoked glass in the windows. I remind myself how it feels in the summer – cool and soothing from the outside heat and glare, and cocooned by the drone of the air conditioning and the swish of the ceiling fans . . . I try to remember – how long it is since I was last here in the summer.

My cousin bursts in. Some waiters bow their elaborately turbaned heads in deferential recognition. She nods slightly in return, looking around to locate me at the same time and, having done so, strides across to my table.

'Have you ordered?'

'No, I was waiting for you.'

'Ah, good,' she returns, putting her bags on the spare chair. 'Sorry I'm a bit late, but I won't bore you with details.' Comfortably installed she picks up the menu and without consulting it, tells me: 'They do very good koftas here and I can recommend the Chicken à la Kiev.'

'I usually have a lightish lunch,' I say looking at the menu.

'Like what?' she asks absently.

'In England it's usually soup or cheese toast and salad . . .'

'You can have that here if you like. You don't have to go by the menu, anything can be ordered. Do you want cheese toast? Of course it's not like your Cheddar cheese, but perfectly decent none the less . . . '

'No, no,' I reply quickly, closing the menu. 'I'm not in England now. I'll have what you have.'

'You're sure?' she returns, and without waiting for a reply raises her hand, clicks her fingers and summons: 'Bearah!'

The waiter appears: a thin old man looking weighed down by his elaborate uniform, his bony face and sad eyes emphasised by the rich red-and-gilt turban and matching cummerbund. He takes the order of two Chicken à la Kiev and walks away with a slight limp.

'I wonder why they dress them in such fancy clothes?' I say, thinking aloud.

'Who? The bearahs?'

'Yes, the waiters.'

'Looks all right to me. It's a uniform. It goes with the job. It's warm and they probably love it.'

'You think so?'

'Oh yes,' replies my cousin with great authority. 'Clothes are expensive and they like to have uniforms. I give all my servants uniforms. A winter one at Divali and summer ones on Baisakhi. They're always very happy and it's part of the family tradition, you know.' To my querying look she replies, 'Oh, yes. Our grandmother always did it. So did Daddy . . . Uncle and everyone. Of course these days it's not so common and lots of people just give old clothes. But we still do it in the old way. In fact it's quite a ritual in our house.'

'Really?'

'Oh, yes. The tailor comes in twice a year for a month, sometimes more, sits out on the veranda, sews away and everything gets done – whatever needs to be made or mended or anything. I pay him a flat rate and give him food and whatever friends or neighbours bring in is extra for him. He does quite well.'

'Sounds most efficient. I'm impressed!'

'Well that's how they used to do it and it means no rushing around for fittings. If he wants to stay on a bit longer and

47

finish other jobs, I let him. He then brings his own tiffin and I give him tea.'

The waiter arrives bearing our food and it suddenly occurs to me why they're called 'bearahs' – bearer! Usha picks up the cone-shaped napkin and expertly unfurls it with a single toss. I try to do the same and end up unfolding it.

'Why are you smiling?' she asks. 'Share the joke.'

'I just worked out that bearahs are called bearers because they bear things!'

'My God, Meera! Now stop all this talk about servants.' She slices the chicken and inspects the rich yellow butter as it spills out on to the plate.

'Tell me about yourself! I mean I haven't seen you for, what is it? How many years?'

'Three.'

'Three? That long? But I spoke to you on the phone in London. Last year, wasn't it?'

I nod.

'So for how long are you here?'

'I've come for three weeks but it feels like the first holiday in three years!'

'No place like home, eh?'

'I suppose so. Yes. Though it would be nice to be at home longer, or to live . . . at home,' I say wistfully.

Usha chews the chicken and nods thoughtfully. 'What about Maya? How is she? You didn't bring her with you?'

'No, I needed to come on my own, but she's fine – spending Christmas with her father – growing up . . . '

The cutlery clinks on the china plates.

'What about you and Martin? The marriage and all? Of course, you don't have to tell me anything if you don't want to. But then again, I am your cousin-sister.'

Words and images swim in my mind – strained, estranged. I think about them, unable to recall the full meaning and implications of the latter. The former sounds suitably ambiguous. 'A bit strained, maybe, but generally things are okay, I suppose.'

'Aren't they all!' exclaims Usha. 'Even the good ones have their strained moments. Though of course in India there are plenty of buffers to prop them up and mitigate the strain.'

'Yes? Like what?'

'Oh I don't know. The whole setup really. The family, appearances, what's done, money, the servants . . . '

'Now it's you talking about servants.'

'Oh, but servants are really important. My servants actually run my house. I couldn't work if they didn't. And they put up with Deepak's outbursts of temper like I could never do. I mean, not only do they manage to humour him out of them, but they even protect the rest of the family from the blast! I mean, you know old Kesru?' I nod. 'Well, as you know, he's been with the family for donkey's years and came to me when Daddy died. Well, you know he still looks after me like a daughter!'

'You're really lucky,' I say, slightly envious at the idea of having a home where I too could still be a child, sometimes.

'And then, of course,' continues Usha, 'there is always the interminable round of weddings – the eternal reminders of family duties, clan, ties, responsibilities, continuity. Watching the sat pathi round the fire and remembering one's own seven steps and their meanings.'

'I see what you mean by buffers.'

'Oh, yes. Lots of buffers. It's all part of the system, part of the whole life here. And this is the wedding season. You're coming to Gautan's wedding of course, aren't you? You know Inderbahi's son?'

'I haven't been invited.'

'Don't be silly! Invited! It's family! You're part of the baraat! You're not expected to wait for an invitation. You're expected to just be there. He probably doesn't even know you're here anyway.'

I smile, feeling rather warmed by the idea of the bonds of belonging.

'I'll be there,' I say cheerfully. 'I wish I could be here all the time!'

'Ah, yes! No place like India.' She pushes aside her empty plate. 'Ah yes,' she sighs. 'That's why I always knew . . . I had to come back.' She dabs her mouth with her napkin. 'And also why I never got involved there.' She catches my eye and continues in a definite tone to contradict any misunderstanding. 'Never got involved in getting work experience in England once I'd finished my studies! Daddy was very clear about it all. He said: "If you stay on, you'll make little roots and then it's a tearing apart." '

A tearing apart! A very apt formulation, I think.

'Of course, it's different for you, you mostly grew up there,' she continues sympathetically.

'Maybe. But it's still a tearing apart. Both ways, from here, from there . . . '

'Tell me,' she says, changing the topic and tone, 'do you want dessert or just coffee?'

'Just coffee.'

She clicks her fingers. 'Bearer, bring us two coffees and take all this away,' she tells the old man who is already clearing the table of dishes and plates.

'Actually, Usha, it was one of the things I wanted to talk to you about.'

She raises her eyebrows questioningly.

'I'm thinking . . . sort of . . . seeing how . . . or if . . . I could come back. You know, exploring possibilities . . . ' Exploring possibilities! It slipped out again. I make a mental note to find another expression. 'I wanted to know what you think.'

'What I think?' She looks at me as at a client with a tax problem – a tax problem requiring careful consideration . . . 'What do I think?' she repeats again. 'Well, I suppose it's really a question of systems.' She looks at me to see if I've understood and, seeing I haven't, continues. 'What I mean is this: each place has its own kind of system. There's one kind of system here and there's another kind of system there. We all get used to the kind of system we're in. Now you have got used to the system over there . . . '

'But surely one can learn and . . . '

'Of course one can learn. But one also has to think what it means. Now you want to come from an organised society into a disorganised society . . . '

'Well, your life sounds pretty organised.'

'Ah yes, but then I'm familiar with the system. How to get it to work – and even then it's not always easy. You see,' she leans forward for emphasis, 'the pace of life here, at least in the big cities, has become very fast. Admittedly not as fast as in the West of course, but still, much too fast for here.'

'Well, for me it's still comparatively leisurely.'

'Comparatively maybe. But only comparatively. You have to see what it means. Take the family for instance. The family is around but they're also all rushing around because it's become so difficult to get anything done. I mean they're there but it's not like it was before, you know, you can't count on them in the same way or just expect things like one could before.'

'I see.'

'You see the old generation and all the strong bonds and joint family ideas and family support – well, they're all getting old and the younger generation wants smaller networks and their own lives. It's difficult to explain, but everything is changing.'

'What generation are we?'

'Well you're younger than me. But I'd say we're in the middle. The younger generation is the twenties and early thirties wallahs. I mean I can still remember the Independence movement – but you were only a baby.'

'I can remember Gandhiji's funeral.'

'You see! I was there too – with you.' She smiles. 'All that's now history. I mean, there were large houses in those days. And this brings me to the next point. Accommodation. Finding a place to live. Have you thought of that? Where would you live? I mean accommodation has become a real problem in Delhi, and I mean a real problem. Apart from being just exorbitantly expensive, it's almost impossible to

51

find.' She takes a gulp of coffee which appears to dislodge some of the impossibles. She continues more sympathetically, 'Well, I suppose it's not impossible and there's a big enough network of people among whom to spread the word to be on the lookout, but again – what you need is also a question of what you're used to . . . which brings me back to my first point.'

'Systems?'

'Systems!'

She finishes off her coffee and pours some more. 'What about Martin and Maya? You have to consider what they're used to. You'll have to think about schools and jobs and . . . but then I suppose you've thought about all that already.' She sips her coffee.

'Well, not really. Or rather thought about it only just a little . . . '

She puts down her cup and laughs good humouredly. 'Well you'll have to think about it more than just a little, Meera. I mean, it's a big move . . . '

'Well, it's just still a vague idea really. Still sort of . . . forming, you know, based on a kind of . . . feeling . . . missing India . . . feeling far away. And there aren't any buffers in my life in the West you know. It's just a lot of stress and strain.'

'Oh, Meera!'

'I just thought I'd look into what was possible and then when I go back . . . see . . . and talk to Maya . . . and . . . '

'You're not thinking of coming on your own are you?'

'No, no. I'd bring Maya. She has to change schools next year, and she's a bit under age, so a year won't make any difference.'

'Is there more to this than meets the eye? Shouldn't I find out what I'm advising you about . . . ' Usha's words put me on the defensive. I give a hollow laugh, to make light of the whole matter and cover my disappointment.

'Oh, it's nothing much really . . . just toying around with the idea. Just trying to see what would be possible.'

'Well, we must talk about it some more. This afternoon I have a meeting I can't miss, but why don't you come for dinner sometime? Come tomorrow. You're not doing anything tomorrow are you? Then come tomorrow!' She clicks her fingers to attract the bearer and asks me simultaneously, 'What's your programme for this afternoon?'

'I need to buy some chappals.'

'Chappals! That's easy! Get them at Cottage. I'll tell you what – I'll drop you at the Cottage Industries on my way. That'll be the best place!' She laughs. 'A bit closer to the system you're used to. You know, like those department stores where you have sections for this and sections for that. But you know Cottage don't you?'

'Yes, of course. Though I must say I'd never thought of it as a department store!'

'Well, it'll be easier than the bazaar. Fixed prices and plenty of choice. Let's go!'

Thirteen

The comparison of the Cottage Industries to a department store makes me smile. Fixed prices, yes, sections for this and that, maybe, but the similarities end there and the initial impact is more like entering Aladdin's cave than the purposeful efficiency of a department store.

The entrance lobby, in keeping with the prevailing spirit of the wedding season, is an ostentatious display of gold glitter, colour and craftsmanship, a mixture of old and new, past and present. Elaborate wedding saris in reds and deep pinks, an ornate antique palanquin hiding a veiled and decked-up bride, a delicately painted wooden horse with an embroidered saddle bearing a bejewelled and brocaded groom. Brass pots, carved wooden chests and more costumes hang in suspended animation.

The shop is set out on three floors. Its different sections, spaciously laid out in the main thoroughfare, disappear at the sides into little labyrinths revealing furs from Kashmir, silks from Madras, sandalwood from Mysore . . . rosewood, ivory, jewellery, cloth, colours, made up into bags, boxes, bedcovers, carpets, clothes, nick-nacks and much more! Arts and crafts from the length and breadth of India all gathered together in stunning splendour – and all seeming to say 'Delhi still rules as the Imperial Capital of Independent India!'

I stroll down the aisles, in and out of the labyrinths, touching, looking, my mind crowding with thoughts, plans, reminiscences, past, present, future, images, colours,

54

sounds, smells . . . Sandalwood visiting cards! What a lovely idea! Could get them for Martin – no, something more useful maybe . . . I suppose I could get them for me, but then what address would I put on them . . . later maybe. And Maya? My little Maya! Best to get her lots of things. Lots of things and so lots of little packets she can open. Yes she'd like that. But what? . . . Gosh, what a nice box . . . Yes, a box . . . could get her a box . . . could get her a box and fill it with bangles! Yes, that's a good idea. Now what sort of a box? An inlaid box? Sandalwood? Lacquered? Leather? Cloth? Carved? All sorts of bangles: silver bangles, brass bangles, enamel bangles, lacquer, bone, beaded, glass . . . glass . . . glass bangles here?

'Upstairs.'

Upstairs . . . let's see, bangles first upstairs. Oh my goodness! Those little brocade purses . . . she'd love one of those. Must get one . . . or two maybe . . . That mango motif . . . very old . . . mango motif on that fragment at the V and A. Fragment from Egypt . . . Indian motif? Did we export cloth to Egypt? That long ago? Could have done I suppose . . . must go and check with the V and A . . .

'You want these?'

'Yes please.' She gathers up the brocade purses I have collected, counts out a total of nine and places them on the counter. As she leans over to make out the bill I watch her two long black plaits swinging on either side of her face. I fumble for my purse wondering how old the oldest piece of cloth in the world is, where it is, and how would one be sure of its age anyway. She hands me my bill and keeps the purses.

'You please pay at cash desk upstairs,' she tells me.

I climb the stairs trying to remember the name of that fabled muslin cloth of old which was very wide and very long and yet fine enough to pass through the ring of a little finger . . . and did the East India Company really cut off the thumbs of the weavers? How ghastly!

'Do you have seventy paisa change?' asks the cashier as I

observe his thumb counting the notes I have given him. I shake my head. 'Never mind.' He smiles as he hands me thirty paisa in stamps.

'But these are . . . What do I do with these?'

'They're stamps,' he tells me.

'I can see they're stamps,' I say a bit irritatedly.

'Good,' he returns. 'You may now collect your parcel at delivery counter downstairs.' He smiles disarmingly.

Downstairs and another queue. As I stand in it and observe that not absolutely everyone sticks to the rules, I reflect about systems. What kind of a system is this . . . a bit of an inbetween system . . . a neither here nor there system. 'The kind of system you're used to!' I collect my parcel, having decided to try my luck in the system of the open bazaar. As I go I notice the section for shoes and sandals close by. I hesitate for only a few seconds as I remember I will choose downstairs . . . pay upstairs . . . collect downstairs – and the system is too complicated for me and outside the sun . . . the sugar-cane juice . . . the street stalls call . . .

As I step out into the crowded street, I follow a family of four walking in front of me and so clearing the way for my free passage. Soon they leave to cross the road, abandoning me to parry my own way down the street, threading through the tourists, shoppers, street vendors and looking for a shoe shop. The first one I find bears a sign saying FIXED PRICE. I stop and smile. The shopkeeper is quick to notice.

'Please, please you come in,' he calls in English. As I step in I wonder if there is something different in my demeanour or dress that makes him address me in English, and, as though reading my thoughts, he continues in Hindi as I enter the shop.

'What can I show you? Please sit down.' I walk around the shop looking at the open-backed sandals we call chappals and decide on a traditional design in natural tan – I want the shade closest to my own skin colour. I sit down and he pulls down a pile for me to try on. As I slip my feet in and out of them or inch them in and pull them out, he busily tells me that they are all fine and assures me that each and every one of them will somehow shrink or stretch in no time to become the perfect fit. In good-humoured exasperation I exclaim: 'But I don't want them to shrink in no time or stretch or whatever else they're supposed to do. What I want to do is take off my old ones now and walk out of this shop with a pair of new ones which fit.'

'Why, yes, of course. Don't worry. I've got another kind which will be just fine. I'll just get them from the other shop. Let me get you a cup of tea while you wait, but I won't be very long.'

Sure enough the sweet tea is not even cool enough to drink before he returns laden with a high pile of boxes. 'This is the very best, very fine,' he says, squatting down and opening up the boxes. The very first one I try on fits. It neither squeezes nor slips but just sits comfortably on my foot. I walk about and decide that the colour too is fine.

'I'll take these. They are nice, much better than the other ones,' I say.

'Oh, yes, of course. These are y'export quality!'

'What does that mean?'

'Y'export quality! Very best quality. Very fine. Export quality! Outside send quality.'

'How much?'

'Seventy rupees!'

'That's expensive.'

'No, no. Very fine, fixed-price export quality,' he repeats.

'What about giving me a very fine fixed price?' He shuffles about for a moment or so and then says, 'Sixty-five rupees.' I don't argue and he looks a bit relieved as I hand him the money and my old heeled sandals.

I walk down the street shuffling my feet to get the full feel of my comfortable new chappals. My heels drag along the ground, and I begin to imagine I'm taking root and almost belong – system or no system. I make my way to a point I would be most likely to find a rickshaw home. I pass a cart selling cards and absently stop to look at them: Christmas

57

cards, New Year cards, Divali greetings, birthdays . . . different kinds and different styles. In one section there is a pile clearly catering for the hippie market. One of them, a photograph in colour, shows a lone figure walking off and away into a tropical sunset . . . the caption inside reads: *I don't know where I'm going but I'm on my way*.

'Three rupees,' says the man. I give them to him and take my card.

'I don't know where I'm going but I'm on my way' and for now I'm on my way down the big shopping street known as Janpath. In my childhood it used to be called Queensway – written as one word. We used to come down here with our pocket money to drink the forbidden sugar-cane juice, buy some aam papad and see if we could pick up a trinket or something in the tent stalls of the Tibetan refugees. Today the same street has been renamed Janpath, 'The People's Way'. The Tibetan tents have become proper bricked shops with iron grilles. Still selling the beads, baubles, bangles and bric-à-brac . . . but enough for today. A rickshaw waits. I get in to drive home. My sari flutters in the wind. I place my feet in such a way as to be able to admire my new chappals as we go along. Export quality! Export quality . . . Ex . . . port . . . qual . . . ity . . . I start to beat a rhythmic time with my foot:

> Export quality smoothly fitting
> Home quality, pinching slipping . . .
> Export quality smoothly . . .

Fourteen

I stop at the market to buy some fruit and knock the silly rhyme out of my head by running in my new chappals and initiating them on the thoroughly home-quality pot-holes and puddles of the colony; and, of course, get them coated with the mandatory cloak of dust – the dust of mother India! Mother India . . . Hail to thee . . . Bande Mataram! I recall an old nationalist song, set to a marchlike tune – we used to sing-march it as children, here, when this same area was a picnic ground – how funny! Is the song still in the air? I stop, as though to catch it:

> Bande Mataram . . . Bande Mataram . . .
> Is miti se thilak karo
> Ye dharthi he palidan ki
> Bande Mataram . . . Bande Mataram . . .

'Come children, let me tell you the glories of India. Mark your forehead with this dust, for this very earth is consecrated . . . Bande Mataram . . . ' And so, clutching my bag of fruit, I march down the tree-lined road of the colony to a new rhythm – this time in four beats.

Bibiji's house is in one of the older, better-established post-Partition colonies and the trees have developed to provide shady avenues. Built around the ruins of old Mogul monuments, in my childhood the area had been a picnic ground, a place to play hide-and-seek. But it had already been ear-marked for development and I remember the discussions about the size of the plots, which had been considered diminutive. In relation to the mansions that had been left behind in Old Lahore these plots had indeed appeared small, yet today the colony did boast mansions when compared to the newer colonies still springing up voraciously all over Delhi, eating into the countryside, consuming villages and transforming the capital into an enormous sprawl.

Each house is different. An assertion of the owner's prize and pride and expressed in a multitude of styles: ornate, utilitarian, eclectic, flat-roofed, tile-roofed, Mogul-domed, pillared, circled, semi-circled, squared, rectangled and all the other possibilities or combinations of possibilities. At each entrance gate a glass nameplate states boldly the owner or tenant of the prize. At night it will be lit up to create a Chinese lantern effect.

I pass an empty unbuilt plot, occupied by squatters in makeshift shacks clinging to the outer walls of the mansions on either side. I stop and look at their rudimentary living conditions: stark, harsh, raw. Bare survival! The children play – sharing their patch with the stray dogs, probably the same ones that howl their complaints during the night. On the balcony of the house opposite, a woman dries her hair, running her fingers through its long tresses to let in the wind and sun. I wonder if she sees the little hutment group? Maybe she sees them as an eyesore, maybe they are casual labour in her house . . . or maybe she doesn't see them at all. If I lived here for long enough would that happen to me? Would I also pass and just not see?

As I approach Bibiji's house I try to catch a glimpse of the luminous pink magenta bougainvillaeas – which I am convinced are richer and brighter than any of the other bougainvillaeas of the colony.

'Meera Bibijiiii!' screams a child's voice and Minoo comes leaping and darting down the road towards me. I stop to watch the ease and wild beauty of her movements. Having

60

reached me she relieves me of my bag of fruit and dances alongside.

'I need to colour Parvati's hair black,' she tells me with a slight pout.

'Then do it,' I reply.

'Can I really do it?'

I laugh. 'Of course you can do it if you want to. She's your doll. I'm not going to take her away. Have you got some colour?'

'Na, na, but there's an ayah in block K and she's got some. I'll show you when it's done.' Her dance becomes more boisterous as she bounds about around me.

'Minoo!' comes Aunt Daya's voice. 'What's this screaming and pouncing and behaving like a junglee? Are you a wild animal or something?' Aunt Daya stands at the gate with her hands on her hips trying to look severe. 'Now walk properly,' she adds as we reach her. In reply Minoo stops in front of her, puts her head down, contorts her mouth into grimaces, rolls her eyes and starts to rub her naked feet against each other.

'She's only a child, Masi,' I smile.

'What child. She's nearly twelve. She can't run loose and wild like a child for much longer and the sooner she learns the better.'

Aunt Daya looks at Minoo who is still rolling her eyes and rubbing her feet. 'You want to grow up into a monkey?' Minoo squeals out a timid giggle in reply. 'Go on then into the house properly; show Meera bibi that you know how.' Minoo walks away, visibly containing her leaps and bounds.

'It's not the child's fault!' mutters Aunt Daya. 'The mother is so busy working all over the place she doesn't seem to have noticed that the girl is growing!' She shakes her head. 'She still allows her to bathe at the open tap – and all the servants' quarters overlook it. I must speak to Bibiji about that. But then, what are the poor people to do when the rich set such a bad example, huh, tell me. Even the servant classes are trying to be Englishised calling their parents Dud-dies and

61

Mum-mies!' She continues to shake her head more vigorously. 'It's the age, you know,' she explains philosophically, looking up towards the sky. 'Kali Yuga: the age of iron! Disintegration of good values! All the sages and scriptures tell about it.'

'So then, Aunty, that settles it, there's nothing we can do and nobody is responsible!' I laugh.

'There you go again. Trying to catch me out with your silly-style jokes! Always something we can do and can be done!'

As the sun has moved away from the garden, so too has Bibiji's durbar. In the house are gathered some of the evening visitors. Among the old ladies, enjoying all the attention, is a young man in jeans. He rises to greet me.

' . . . these days everyone is wanting to go into business. Even the most respectable people,' Mrs Malhotra is explaining and everyone else nodding their agreement.

'You don't recognise me,' says the young man.

'Of course she recognises you, Gulu!' bursts in Aunt Daya, ever protective.

'How could she not recognise her own cousin!' adds Mrs Tandon.

'You've grown!' I reply rather stupidly and laugh. 'That's what everyone used to say to me whenever I used to come back to India – "You've grown!" I must say I never thought the day would come when I'd be saying that myself to somebody.'

'He's nearly finished college. Soon we'll have to start looking for a girl,' Aunt Daya teases.

'Nothing doing. No way! Not yet! Never!' Gulu is clearly adept at these good-humoured protestations.

'That's what they all say to start with, but sooner or later they all get married.'

'God willing . . . '

'Yes, but nowadays the new generation have their own ideas.'

' . . . people getting divorced and married again . . . '

' . . . it's happening in the best of families . . . '

' . . . it's all due to Westernisation . . .' 'Urbanisation . . .' 'Modernisation . . . ' 'Consumerisation . . . ' 'No, no! It is the fault of the politicians . . . '

'So, what are your plans?' I ask my young cousin.

'I want to go to America and take a business studies course,' he replies smartly.

'Business studies,' comes Bibiji's hitherto silent voice. 'Everyone nowadays wants to do business studies! This is what they imagine we need in India today! Lots of American-trained business . . . whatever they are called – business wallahs?' She shakes her head as she writes. Gulu smiles, gracious but determined. 'In the old days, the best young men all wanted to go into the services.'

'But now even the services are demoralised . . . '

'All the professions are demoralised . . . '

'Did you buy the chappals?' asks Bibiji.

'Aahaah, ye-es!' Aunt Daya exclaims as though she has retrieved something from a long-lost memory store. 'The chappals! Did you buy the chappals? Let's see. Show us all.'

It is now my feet that form the centre of focus. My new chappals still shine in spite of the thin coat of consecrated dust.

'Very nice!'

'Yes, very nice!'

'Kolapuri?'

'Leather?'

'Nice colour . . . '

'How much?'

'Yes, how much were they?'

'Sixty-five rupees.'

'Sixty-five rupees!'

'So much!'

'That's too much!'

'Very expensive!'

'Sixty-five!'

'Did you make him come down?'

'Well, he did have cheaper ones.'

'Then why didn't you get the cheaper ones, rani?' Aunt Daya sounds concerned.

'He said these were more expensive because they were export quality and the leather was cured differently.'

'That's what they all say!' Gulu laughs.

'And they were more comfortable . . . '

'They're very nice, rani, and it is important to wear comfortable shoes,' Bibiji interjects. Everyone agrees.

'Everything is "export" these days . . . ' ventures Mrs Anand.

'Export quality! Business studies! Never marry! That's the new generation. The old values!' Everybody has a say and the conversation – hardly a conversation – the talk, rather, is like a juggling act in which new balls keep being thrown in, tossed about and lost . . .

Gulu tries to explain his twenty-one-year-old wisdom of how times have changed, how India must keep up with the international developments . . . how it is an eighth industrial power which must now leap into the twenty-first century and how important it is to understand about business and finance capital . . . As young Gulu elucidates the assembly extrapolates and the talk goes everywhere.

'This export quality is very bad,' Aunt Daya confides as she moves across and sits down beside me. 'You know that cloth we got for the parcel? Well it used to be the cheapest cloth, the very cheapest cloth which the poor people would buy for their use. Now, it's all exported!' She raises her eyebrows and widens her eyes. 'All exported! They use it to make clothes to send out and now the poor people can't afford to buy it.'

'What do they do?' I ask.

'What can they do? Nothing. Respectable people, even people from old families like ours . . . respectable people have given up their secure and worthwhile jobs in the services and opened up little clothes factories in their garages. It's become a – what do you call it? – a crazy?'

64

'A craze?'

'Craze . . . crazy, same thing. It's all crazy anyway!'

' . . . in the old days people used to go abroad to become doctors, engineers . . . ' the balls are still being tossed around.

'We can do all that here now, Burri Aunty. People even come from there to go to medical school here.'

'And do you know medical colleges in India have become so expensive that ordinary middle-class people can't afford to pay the fees.'

'But what about schools, leave alone the fees, you have to pay a premium to get in . . . '

'It has become impossible to live on a salary . . . '

' . . . that is why so many people are going into business . . . '

'Isn't it all just Kali Yuga?' I toss my ball into the group . . . but it is not picked up, and is lost . . . or maybe it is suspended to be pulled down at another time.

Like a pre-timed clock the well-oiled routine clicks into place. Chandu appears squeaking his way in and out of the kitchen as he makes the arrangements for tea. Maie comes and squats down at Bibiji's feet and starts to massage and rub her legs soothingly. She will do this until the tea is brought in, whereupon she will go and have her own tea before getting things ready for Bibiji's walk. There is something immeasurably comfortable and soothing about routine . . . and when it's all done for you – it is luxury!

'I was remembering how we used to come here for picnics sometimes when I was small.' Bibiji sips the tea from her teacup and nods her head.

'That was such a long time ago. But even then we knew it was going to be developed. It was already in the master plan.'

'The what?'

'The Delhi master plan,' explains Gulu. 'They made a plan of how and when they were going to develop different areas in Delhi. And Dad said that some of these government big

65

shots would find out and buy up and then make a bomb. Isn't that right, Burri Aunty?'

'Some people made a . . . bomb as you call it.'

'How much was land in those days?'

'Three rupees a yard, but you weren't supposed to get more than one plot per person. So people would get plots in the names of children, grandchildren . . . '

'Adopted children, dogs and cats . . . ' adds Gulu playfully.

'And what's a plot worth now, Bibiji?'

'Now, rani! Ohh! Now it must be worth about two thousand rupees a yard!'

'What! Two thousand! It can't be a rupee under three thousand at the very least.' Gulu speaks in his worldliest of tones.

'Gosh!' I exclaim. 'That means it's gone up a thousand per cent.'

'What thousand per cent!' Gulu laughs. 'Much more than that! If it was a thousand per cent it would be only thirty rupees a yard.'

'I don't understand.'

'If you want to calculate it in percentages then three to a thousand is an increase of about one hundred thousand per cent.'

'I understand even less.'

'None of us understand the way this country is going,' says Bibiji, taking the walking stick that Minoo has just handed her, and levering herself out of her armchair. 'Give me my shawl,' she tells Maie who is already starting to drape it on her shoulders. 'Come, rani,' she tells Aunt Daya. 'You want to come too, baby?' she asks me, and we all leave.

As we stroll through the colony, Aunt Daya gives me a guided tour of who from Old Lahore lives where, if they're there, or if they've let their property to live elsewhere. Which architect they chose to design their house, what it cost, if there have been any weddings or scandals in the family . . .

66

'Daya! One thing I don't understand. You keep telling us how unworldly you are – eat dry roti, bathe in Gangaji and yet you clutter your mind up with a surprising amount of the most useless information!'

'I was just telling Meera . . . '

'And what does Meera want to know all this for?'

'It will give Meera bhen a feel of India,* Burri Aunty,' suggests Gulu.

Bibiji shakes her head as we walk along for a while in silence.

'Did Usha have anything to say?' she asks.

'You saw Usha ben? I haven't seen her for at least a year. Not since the last family wedding. I'll probably see her at both this year.'

Gulu and Aunt Daya quicken their pace carrying away with them a discussion on the advantages and disadvantages of getting married young.

Bibiji puts her hand on my shoulder as I tell her about my day. When we meet up again at the house I am telling Bibiji that I want to get some bangles for Maya. All advise me where to go to and which is the 'very best place'. In the end it is agreed that the Tuesday fair at the Hanuman Mandir would be the most suitable.

'Go with Sita. She goes there regularly. She will take you. Yes, go with Sita.'

Aunt Daya nods her head – in agreement, but also, it turns out, in time – as she bursts out into a devotional song by Meerabai, the great fourteenth-century poetess. Bibiji fingers her mala, Maie smiles, closes her eyes and presses Bibiji's feet to the rhythm. In the kitchen Chandu's pans clink and clang. Gulu looks out and listens to the cars. He crosses his legs a bit restlessly, probably wishing that his parents would arrive soon to pick him up. I sink back into the sofa and think: 'Dear India!'

Fifteen

'It's all right for you to go by taxi. But coming back is a different matter. Have you arranged with Usha about getting home?'

'I'm sure it will be all right, Bibiji. She must have a reliable taxi stand where she lives as well.'

Bibiji is outraged. She shakes her head and puts away her writing so as to free her hands and emphasise her point. 'Rani, I don't want you coming back in a taxi from there. You must tell Usha to arrange to have you dropped: really Meera you must promise me you'll do that.'

'Aunty, I'll do that. Really I will.'

'And don't come back in a taxi from there. If Usha can't drop you home then you take the number of Bhagwan Das's taxi rank and he'll send a car. Come, I'll write the number down.' She finds a piece of paper and starts to do so, 'Bhagwan Das is absolutely reliable. I've known him since he was a boy. His grandfather used to run a tonga taxi service in Old Lahore. Here's the number. He's open all night, and all his taxi drivers are trustworthy.' She hands me the paper, still muttering under her breath. 'You girls! This is not London or America and girls don't take taxis and wander around on their own at night!'

I take the paper from her, and squeeze her hand as I do so. 'Aunty, you have my word that I'll make absolutely sure that I am dropped safely home at a reasonable hour.'

Usha's small driveway is crammed with cars spilling on to the pavement. Clearly this will not be the dinner tête-à-tête I was led to expect but a fully-fledged dinner party – what is called 'just a few friends over, informal "doo"!' Snacks, six or seven dishes, a couple of desserts and plenty of booze. In any case it will be more elaborate than the most elaborate 'doo' that I ever do – the annual celebration of Divali, my Indian evening of the year. The divide is more than just of space, time – it's lifestyles.

'I say, Usha. She's come! She's arrived! She's here. Tell them she's here!' says Usha's husband, Deepak, on opening the door. 'The old aunts are on the phone giving Usha a hard time about your coming and going.' I start to make my second-nature apology. He pre-empts it. 'No need to apologise, we're used to all this. We live here.'

Innocently said, the last remark feels like a kick. 'We live here.' Indeed! And I don't! I am just a visitor . . . a passing stranger. In the background Usha's voice coos on the telephone, ' . . . yes, Aunty . . . don't worry, Aunty . . . yes, of course I'll be over to see you very soon. Promise. I just said, promise. Okay then. 'Bye Aunteee.' Her voice lilts up as she ends the conversation and replaces the receiver.

'Hi, Meera,' she exclaims in the boisterous tone of party *bonhomie*. 'That was the old aunts making sure I would send you home in one piece. And what are you doing just standing here? And without a drink? You mean to say my husband hasn't even got you a drink? I say, Deepak . . . Deepak? The door and the drinks are his domain . . . everything else is mine!' She laughs. 'Come, let's go and help ourselves in his domain, since he's nowhere to be seen. I really need a drink after that call. The old aunts really take the cake with all their worrying. My God one would imagine that Delhi was the wild of the wilds . . . not the capital of India!'

'I wasn't expecting a dinner party . . . '

'Naah. Don't be silly. It's just a few friends over. Quite informal! It's the season.'

'The what?'

'The season! During the cool season everyone socialises, shops, stocks up . . . it's the time for getting repairs done, clothes made . . . for meeting people . . . dinners . . . Will you have whisky?'

'Why not,' I reply. She hands me what looks like a rather large measure and leads me into the room.

'It's just an informal get-together. I thought it would be nice for you to come along and meet people, get a feel of things.'

'Systems?'

Usha laughs. 'Exactly! Systems. Now you're getting the idea!'

The evening is just starting. In the room, five or six people sit, stand, chat, move around and the room exudes the comfort of affluence and familiarity. I look around to see if I can find a familiar face, and recognise only the warm and weathered face of old Kesru, the cook. I go up to greet him before Usha whirlwinds me through 'the gang' – all elegantly dressed and professional, successful or rich, and all of whom say a long 'Hiii' to 'Cousin Meera from London' as we step in and out interrupting conversations about cricket, politics, shopping, tailors, prices. In between she fills me in with titbits of gossip and I keep colliding with the gentle eyes of old Kesru.

'In the plane I was remembering those long lemon drinks Kesru used to make us during our Monopoly games.'

'And water melon with ice!' Usha echoes my nostalgia in her tone. 'Well you'll be seeing Romi later on . . . do you remember him? He used to play with us too. Businessman now. Goes abroad quite a lot. It will be good for you to meet him. I say, Vijay,' she calls a passing guest, 'have you any idea where Deepak is? Be a darling and have a look . . . or get Meera another drink and I'll go and have a look.' She hands him my glass, which, to my surprise is quite empty!

My head slightly light, the idea of another drink feels self-indulgent. I sink back comfortably into the sofa from where all I can see is the smoke drifting up to lock itself round the still ceiling fans. The season! Cool, comfortable camaraderie, and wouldn't it be nice to be here – always.

70

'Your drink.'

'Ah, thanks.' I sit up. 'I'm glad you haven't given me too much . . .'

'Is this enough? Would you like some more?'

'No, no! No more! I think I've probably had enough as it is!'

'I'm Vijay. I work with Usha's firm of accountants. And you're Usha's cousin on a visit to Delhi?' He sits down beside me, a fresh-looking young man who can't be more than twenty-three I decide . . .

'Yes, that's right,' I reply and try to emulate the sing-song Delhi 'Hiii' and decide that it doesn't sound quite right. Vijay smiles, rather knowingly I think.

'Everyone says "Hi" in India don't they?'

'Well, no. Not everyone and not everywhere. Not where I come from.'

'Where's that?'

'Hyderabad. You know of Hyderabad?'

'Yes, of course. I'm not a tourist. I've been to Hyderabad. And Secunderabad and the caves at Ajanta and Ellora caves . . . just like a tourist!' We both laugh.

'And now you're settled in London?'

'Oh no, no, not settled!' I reply. He looks surprised and I am taken aback at the vehemence of my tone. 'What I mean is that . . . well yes, I do live in London, but "settled" somehow sounds so . . . so definite . . . so secure, so comfortable, so . . . sort of self-contained.'

'I see.' He looks at me kindly.

'Yes. And I don't feel any of those things. In fact, I miss India . . . and now that I'm here I'm realising how much! I'd love to be here.'

'But your family are there?'

'No, not any more.' I sip my drink. 'Well, that's to say, I only have a husband and daughter there.'

'Only?' He laughs.

'I didn't mean it to sound quite like that! They're certainly not unimportant.' I try to make light of my remark. 'It's just

71

that being here, I associated family with my parents. They returned to India you see, my mother wasn't too well . . . but now they're both gone. This is my first visit since my father's death.'

He nods his head in sympathy but says nothing. I am grateful for the silence.

'I suppose it's the difference of the family where you're looked after and the family where you do the looking after.'

'I understand exactly what you mean.'

'How could you,' I reply rather accusingly.

'I have an older sister. She feels the same and tells me about it. Though I'm probably the only person she does. It's more difficult for her because she has to live with her in-laws. I have to be here for another eight months, so I also feel far from home. And Delhi you know, is – '

'But you're still in India!' I interrupt. 'The sounds, the smells, the life, the fascination of the place! It's still where you belong! In London I am a stranger and constantly feel a stranger. It's very lonely and I seem to have lost my way.'

'What about your husband?'

'Oh, he's there. He has his work. It's his country. He's just got a new job in fact, and it involves moving towns . . . and that's when it all started to happen.'

'What?'

'Well . . . he got this new and better job and we were all going to move and then, we decided that it would be better to wait for Maya to finish her last year at school, because next year she'll be eleven and will have to change schools in any case. So the two of us stayed on, and Martin – that's my husband – moved, and I got a full-time job so as to manage the two mortgages.'

'And so you still haven't moved?'

'No. There's still time . . . but also, I'm not ready. It was the first time in years that I was on my own . . . and I found myself thinking of a lot of things: where I was going, what I was doing, how I'd come to be where I was, and feeling disconnected. Being in India has made it all more intense, and made me feel that I need to come back here to make it all fit and make me whole . . . ' I gulp down the rest of my drink and then try to absorb what I have just said . . . coming back to make me whole . . .

'Dinner! I say, dinner everybody,' Usha's voice brings me back to the room, the party, the season, the smoke-filled room and a rude awakening that I have been talking too much, too close to the raw edge . . . to a total stranger . . . with a soothing presence . . . I start to stammer and, of course, apologise: 'Gosh, I'm sorry going on like this. I must have had a bit too much to drink.' Usha appears, to save the day, distributing plates and tearing people away from their conversations by directing them to the table with a 'Food's hot . . . come on . . . Food's hot.' Vijay's reply remains unspoken and I am left with the undigested realisation of what I have just said . . .

'Romi's come,' calls out Deepak, back at his duties by the door.

'Late yar!' They greet each other.

'What late! It's just Indian standard time!'

'Some excuse! And such a lame one!'

The room has become crowded, the conversation centred over and around the one-way traffic of the dining-table buffet. 'I say have you heard . . . ' 'No! What really . . .' 'What a nice sari . . .' 'They should just establish president's rule and flush them out . . . it's these Indians over there who are the troublemakers . . . once they've chosen to leave they should just leave . . . this half foot here half foot there is no good . . .' 'The only place you can find a good tailor these days is at Usha's . . .' 'Satish is trying to get a Congress ticket . . . the best investment . . . very best investment . . . '

'I say you were a long time in London this time, Romi.'

'It's the ethnic traffic, yar! Had one hell of a time getting a booking, just full with ethnic traffic. Had to pull strings here and there . . . '

My inner state and the outer world collide. I take my half-full plate to slip away to a quiet corner of the room. I catch Kesru's eyes and want to cry. Suddenly the room feels oppressive, the smoke suffocating. I fiddle with the food and wonder if my legs would carry me to the kitchen.

'I say rat-catcher, hear you've taken to London mice! Indian rats too tough for you now?' Romi laughs down at me; every inch of him, down to his ringed, manicured fingers, asserts a pampered prosperity. 'You're certainly looking well on the mice diet. What is it? Twelve, fifteen years? And you look exactly the same.'

'Thank you.'

He laughs loudly, drawing attention. ' "Thank you" she says. I remember now we used to tease you and call you English Missy and you'd get so upset.'

'That was a long time ago, Romi.' I wince at how curt, cutting and very English my reply sounds.

'I say, tell me one thing,' comes an interruption. 'You all must be knowing, but why do these Indians in London call themselves black?' She turns around to explain her question to the two or three people who have gathered around us drawn by Romi's laughter. 'You know, when I went to London recently, it was after some ten years that I hadn't been, and I met these Indians who kept saying things like "Black people like us". I said to them straight, "Now look here, baba, don't call me black. I mean where am I black . . . do I look like a habshi?" '

'You mean the Indians call themselves black? Surely not . . .'

'No, not all of them but some of them do. Some of them call themselves black.'

'What about you? O fair one, do you call yourself black?' To my dismay the question is addressed to me. As I wonder how to answer it a familiar voice breaks through the laughter.

'In England they have a different situation and the word is not used to mean a colour, or darkness, but a shared identity . . .' It is Vijay's voice, but his attempted explanation is soon dispersed in peals of laughter and chatter. The

74

question wasn't supposed to be answered.

'How did you know all that?' I ask him later.

'I was in England for two years.'

'You didn't tell me!' He laughs. I join him. 'Well I suppose I didn't give you much of a chance.'

'No, not at all. You needed to talk and I do hope that everything works out for you in the best way.'

I smile and look around the room trying to locate Usha for my lift home.

'Remember also. There are many Indias!'

'What was that?'

'I said, there are many Indias.'

'Yes. That's what I heard. My father used to say something like that. Thanks for reminding me.'

Sixteen

The smell of sandalwood tells me that I have overslept, the crackle-grate sound of the broom next door that the bedrooms have been vacated and that Bibiji has taken her position in her great chair, all set for the day to unfold. For unfold it surely will, just as surely as the sun will rise, and shine, and set, without a twilight, at the same time, as it does all the year round. Against this steady backdrop of the predictable and the routine, every other event, however small, is like a piece of drama: the arrival of the postman – will there, or will there not be any letters? Who will, and who will not call? The telephone for a bit of gossip maybe, and then, if all else fails, the strolling fruit- or vegetable-seller can be counted upon to provide a sort of entertainment, by being called in and proposed a preposterous price for his wares, the ensuing haggle followed by the poor man's display of indignation. If Aunt Daya is around she'll protest . . . but then that too will provide part of the entertainment. For Aunt Daya, as a young widow, has known her share of humiliation even though she might have been protected from the brunt of it by having been able to return to her own family, take back her maiden name, finish her education and lead an independent life. Quite fortunate, really, but still always under the tutelage of the elders of the family, of course, of whom the only ones now left are Bibiji and Aunt Pushpa. Indeed there really are so many Indias!

The bucket of bath water is still hot and Minoo I can hear has moved into my room.

'You really should wait until I've got ready and out before you start sweeping in the room,' I tell her on coming out of the bathroom. She throws down her reed broom in reply, startling up a little cloud of dust and smiling disarmingly.

'I'm not surprised you have to keep sweeping the rooms so often, all you do is shift the dust around.'

'But Meera bibiji it's always there.'

'But of course it's always there since you never remove it.'

'But even then it will come back, bibiji! I'll sweep it away and it will come back because it's everywhere and . . . always there.' She smiles pure enchantment.

'Ach, Minoo!' I exclaim as I leave the room thinking about the many Indias.

'Come, come, sit, sit.' Bibiji greets me as usual without raising her head from her industrious writing in what looks like a newly started old diary. I look over her shoulders to see the date – 1958 – and watch the formation of the miniscule letters . . .

'Ram ram, rani, ram ram. Today you will have some fresh cow's milk, I can get you fresh cow's milk!' says my aunt Daya transiting through the room hurriedly and not waiting for a reply.

'Does ram have any meaning other than being the name of Sri Rama, Bibiji?' I ask as I sit down.

'Oh yes, of course! Ram,' Bibiji takes a deep breath, savouring the sound and the question. 'Ram means . . . that which dwells in all . . . that . . . which permeates the whole universe . . . ram, ram, ram . . . ' She sings the word softly for a while in time with her writing . . .

'That which is everywhere and always there?' I tease.

'Yes, that which is everywhere and always there.'

'Everywhere and always there is what Minoo just called the dust!'

'Oh the dust too . . . it permeates through the dust too!'

'So then everything can be called Ram . . . '

77

'But of course! Everything is ram . . . '

Chandu brings me a cup of tea as Aunt Daya once again transits through the room mumbling away about cow's milk as she hurries out of the door.

'So, tell me now. How was the dinner?' asks Bibiji once quiet has returned.

'Well, it turned out to be a party with a dozen or so people.'

'Accha? The food must have been very good. Kesru's a very good cook.'

'Yes, the food was good.'

'And Usha dropped you home?'

'No, she didn't. She sent me with a friend of hers.'

Bibiji raises her eyebrows questioningly.

'A Raj Swarup,' I reply.

'Swarup? . . . Raj Swarup? Anand Swarup's son? Is his father a chartered accountant?'

'I forgot to ask him what his father did, Bibiji,' I tease, 'but I think he said he was a journalist.'

'Ah ha ha! It's the same one! I remember now. Anand Swarup's son is a journalist. Only son! It's the same! And his mother's name is . . . Rita.' She pauses and the small reminiscing smile which lights up her face briefly flashes into a definitely mischievous look – her eyes sparkle, her single tooth gleams – all the signs through which I know there is a story there waiting to be told . . .

'So. What's the story? Tell me the story?'

'No, nothing. What story?' She looks at me with wide-eyed innocence and the sun even conspires to make her silver hair shine like a halo!

'I know there's a story, Aunty . . . In India they're like ram . . . everywhere!'

'Ram . . . ram . . . ram.' She mutters under her breath, hoping maybe that the invocation will help to dispel and contain the flood of recollections . . . but ram is playful and our world is his Leela, the cosmic game. In spite of her struggles, the smile flickers and flashes and the mischievous tooth will not be contained. Those little particles of dust which carry in their memory this particular story will combine and the story will emerge. A bit of coaxing though will help.

'Come on, Aunty! You know how I love stories, and I'm never here for long enough to get my fill. When I was little I would curl up next to Mama and ask her to tell me stories about India.'

'Hai, rani.' Bibiji shakes her head to be reminded of her niece. Well, it's not really much of a story . . . nothing at all, just a little incident.'

'Let's hear it!' I make myself comfortable and put away my empty cup.

'Well, darling,' she starts. 'In the old days, in Lahore, in Old Lahore . . . '

I soak in and savour the words . . . the tell-tale cues . . . 'In Old Lahore . . . ' Yes, yes, this is how the good stories of the family begin.

' . . . well the young men would have to be sent off to England to study. Naturally, it was always a big event – and even though we knew it had to be done and was in the best interests of our boys, the families would be worried and upset. In those days it was very far away. There weren't any aeroplanes, they had to go by ship, and so it often meant a separation of three or four years, and more if they went for medicine or law. So, before they'd leave, we – all the women that is – would fast, do paat, puja, prayers and feed the fish so that . . . '

'Feed the what?'

'The fish. Feed the fish.' As I still look bewildered, she explains: 'Why, yes. Didn't you know? Well, we would make a big degchi – a big vessel – of sweet rice and carry it down to the nearest river and feed the fish with it to invoke the protection of water and life – so that the fish in the sea would safeguard our boys on their long voyage and would get them there safely. After that we would come home and pray for their wellbeing, that they should be successful in their studies

79

and then . . . ' she pauses to find the appropriate formulation, 'you know, come back safely and settle down in India.'

'Settling down' I knew meant getting married. 'Of course, Aunty,' I reply sympathetically. She looks relieved and puts away her notebook and pen.

'You see now, times have changed, changed a great deal from those days. You young people have more control over your lives and it's a different world. But in those days, we all lived in big joint families, the British were our rulers and life in England too was very different. We were naturally anxious – after all, our boys were going very far away, they might be lonely, exposed to different ways and temptations of all kinds and then, who knows . . . they might in their loneliness get engaged in a . . . well, you know, an unsuitable match.' She quickly stops.

Since her self-image and dignity will not allow her to be accused of narrow-mindedness, and she would not wish to offend me, she hastens to add: 'Of course, mind you, it was not always unsuitable. Sometimes, many times in fact, it worked out very well. For instance, look at Helga Das, Narpat Das's wife, you know Arun Das's mother – I mean look how well she has fitted in; and she even speaks Hindi without an accent, and not just Hindi; she even speaks Punjabi! Or take your own Aunty Mavis, who married your Uncle Giri. No, no. Sometimes it worked out very well. But still, for us womenfolk, especially our mothers, it was always a worry – and a fear – because, you see, a lot of the older women didn't even speak English!' She stops being defensive and adds indignantly, 'It was bad enough having our own boys coming back and behaving like sahibs and telling everyone what to do!'

Bibiji is now well launched as she settles back more comfortably in the chair before resuming. 'Now, Anand Swarup's father, that's to say your Raj's grandfather, was the doctor to our family, as well as to many of the other big Lahore families. And he was really very bad.' She shakes her head at the memory of it. 'Now he was a very good doctor, no doubt about that, but, such a . . . ' she tries to find the word, ' . . . such a wicked man! Such bad taste! So cruel! He would come around and chide people about their sons' departures, come and tell the ladies that they should start learning English in preparation to meet their daughters-in-law! Then he would frighten them with all sorts of made-up stories about life in England and they would all get so distressed. Really his mocking was in very bad taste. So bad, in fact, that when your uncle was in England we would think twice about calling the doctor sahib when we were ill in case we would feel worse after his visit!' She shakes her head and laughs.

'Then, one day, we heard that the doctor sahib had not been seen around. No one had seen him at the club. He hadn't been seen in the Gardens or strolling in the Mall Road. No one had seen him anywhere! And then the news spread around Lahore, that the doctor sahib's son Anand, that's your Raj's father, had suddenly disappeared – had eloped with a Christian girl.' She stops for effect, 'Now the doctor sahib had already taunted his friends beyond endurance, so it was unlikely that they would show him much sympathy. In any case he didn't dare show his face anywhere. For ten days, he wasn't seen at the club and his assistant attended to all his calls, and we heard that he had locked himself in the house – and do you know what he did?'

I shake my head. 'No, what?'

'Well, we heard that the doctor sahib was so upset that he neither ate nor drank – just cried – and as he had no one to give him any sympathy, he would sit in front of the mirror and just cry, and cry, and cry, and then stop, console himself, and then start all over again, to cry and cry and cry . . . ' My great-aunt's face beams with an unabashed smile of satisfaction as she reaches out for her diary and pen and starts, once again to write ' . . . ram . . . ram, ram . . . ' Slowly the smile is contained, the mischievous tooth tucked away, but the sparkle in the eyes remains.

'I've got the milk, fresh cow's milk, here's your milk,

Auntyji.' Aunt Daya places a glass of milk on the two-tiered table. 'I've put your milk on the table, come and drink it, it's fresh cow's milk.'

'What's so special about this milk?'

'It's fresh cow's milk.'

'And what's the other milk? Buffalo?'

'What, buffalo!' returns my aunt contemptuously. 'What do we know? Buffalo? Soya? Water? All put into a bottle and told us now milk. What do we know? But this, is fresh cow's milk.' She looks dreamy. 'From Mrs Verma's cow, the cow I feed . . . and cow's milk is the best food in the world . . . drink it up.'

On the table is set a cup of hot milk, its film just beginning to form . . . its smell is strong, almost pungent, familiar . . . evocative: 'Who's going to drink the lovely dudu? Who's going to drink the lovely milk? Is the queen on the glass going to drink it up . . . ?'

'Nooooo.'

'Then whooo?'

'Mee–aah!'

'Meera. Meera's going to drink the dudu for Mama.'

'Ma–mah!'

I pull my chair back abruptly from the smell . . . the images evoked . . . the milk . . . the memory . . .

'Bibiji, the milk's too strong. I can't drink. But I don't want to upset Aunt Daya if I leave it.'

'Na, rani, leave the milk if you don't want it – it can be made into dahi or paneer. Do you want something else?'

'No. I slept so late that I can wait for lunch. I think I'll go out for a little walk.'

'Rani?' Bibiji's voice is deep and definite. 'Are you all right?'

'Oh, yes!' I reply. I walk down the drive with a forced lightness aware that Bibiji's eyes are following me . . .

How strange that just the smell of milk should evoke such old and forgotten memories – probably my earliest – of drinking

82

milk with my . . . mother. I had a special glass with a picture on it . . . a picture of a queen . . . like the queen in a pack of cards?

The footsteps that have been racing up behind me slow down and stop as a panting Minoo lolls and leaps by my side.

'Bibiji sent you?'

'Na, na, na,' she protests too ardently.

My great-aunt, I know, has sixth-sensed something and set Minoo at my heels to watch over me . . .

'Then why did you come when you haven't finished your work?'

' . . . just . . . I just . . . I came to tell you about the doll!' She adds the last, delighted to have found a good reason.

'So. You've coloured her hair?'

'No, the ayah I told you about said that we'd do it after Christmas. She wants to keep her and put her in the manger and then after Christmas she'll make her hair for me.'

'Isn't the ayah a bit grown up to be playing with little girls' dolls?'

'No, no, why? She's a Christian, nah, isn't she? And she wants to make the doll into baby Jesus and put him in the manger and she said that Jesus has golden hair so she'll keep him Jesus until after Christmas and then make her hair for me . . . '

'And transform her into Parvati.'

'Ha, yes, that's it.'

I laugh as I think of what I will tell Maya about the Indian adventures of her doll . . .

'Meera bibi, what was the doll's name before . . . '

'You mean when Maya had her? She used to change their names quite a lot but I remember she was first called Lovely Sunshine.'

'Lovely sunshine?'

'That's right, Lovely sunshine. You know over there where we live the sun doesn't shine every day.'

'You mean, some days you have no sun?'

'More than that! Sometimes we don't see any sunshine for

weeks, even months!' I shudder myself at the recollection. 'And sometimes, like now, the day will end at tea time, at tea time it will get dark . . . '

'You mean at tea time it will be night time?'

'That's right.' I am amused at Minoo's increasing bewilderment.

'No sun, all dark, no dust, no set time. Haii, Meera bibiji, I wouldn't like to go there! Why don't you come back and live here!'

'And no little sweeper girls either. All the little girls of your age are in school.'

'Hai, Meera bibiji. You all come back and live here and I'll come and sweep for you. Would you like to come back and live here, Meera bibiji?'

'Yes, Minoo, I would.'

'Then come back, Meera bibiji. Come back. Or don't go back now and send for them to come here!'

'Ahh, Minoo! I wish it was as easy as that! Come, let's go home.'

Seventeen

My dear friend,

I have come into my room to be on my own. I am feeling a
bit vulnerable and raw . . . Usha's party was disappointing
and I felt lonely. I drank too much and blurted out I don't
know what – but too much – to a perfect stranger! And
now this morning, the smell of the hot milk plummeted me
into my early childhood – into a flood tide of forgotten
memories and emotions as I saw and smelt and felt my own
mother! Her soft cool hands pushed away a lock of hair
from my face as she coaxed me to drink my milk . . .

It's difficult to describe, but there's something about
India, or being in India, where one has the feeling that . . .
nothing goes away, and that nothing has gone, and that
somehow everything just lingers, disappears, reappears,
co-exists, merges – like the dust! 'Everywhere and always
there' like little Minoo said! Quite true! In a Western
metropolis, with its asphalt, concrete and glass, one can
contain all this and create an illusion of man's omnipotence, of linear time and the technological God! But here,
in India, dust defies any such idolatry. It permeates
everywhere like a continuous and continual reminder of
the eternal omnipresence and final omnipotence of nature
and time.

Sometimes I watch the dancing particles and wonder
how old they are. Are they as old as the city itself? And
how old is that? For the city of Indraprashtha from the

ancient epic Mahabharata is supposed to have stood here –
where Delhi stands today . . . Could the dust of then still
linger – like the thousands and thousands of stories from
the old epic which are still told and retold as they have
been for some four or five thousand years? Stories and
dust! India! Millions of stories, and always dust!

I've been meeting my relations and trying to get an idea
of how I could return. Tomorrow I see Savitri, wife of my
elusive cousin Ravibhai who has become a government
jet-setter and whom I remembered on the plane, but
probably won't see as he flew in only to fly out again. So
far everything has been as elusive as Ravibhai – everything
eludes me, the questions, the answers, the something I am
looking for as I get increasingly lost in longing, memories
and stories. India is so full of contradictions, such a jumble
of possibilities, the clock is ticking . . . my time here will
draw to an end . . . as yet I have not managed to work out
quite how, where and in what particular groove or system I
could slot in.

Eighteen

The car rattles through the colony, bouncing over the pot-holes and on reaching the highway, lunges into the stream of traffic like a predator pouncing on prey. Propped up on cushions in the driving seat, my delicate-looking cousin-sister is transformed: viewing the road rapaciously from her vantage point as she dodges and hoots and swerves her way through the medley that forms the traffic of the highway: cars, cows, taxis, trucks, buses, bullock carts, hand carts, horse carts, cycles, scooters, autorickshaws, pedestrians, donkeys, dust, all claiming their right of way as the drama of power and privilege is asserted – not always without protest I note, as the scooter rickshaw we have been hooting and almost bumping eventually swerves aside, belching out a huge spurt of filthy black smoke, timed so that its full impact hits us just as we overtake. The driver throws us a glacial look, quite lost on my cousin-sister who is already racing ahead to claim her next victim.

In the back seat, my nephew and niece argue as to which of the identical Toblerones I have given each of them is larger. To my look they smile shyly as I admire their sparkling, bright-button-eyed beauty! This is their outing treat, to a special hotel, built for the Asian Games, which serves a favourite Italian-style ice cream.

'Meer-unty! Look look look look look Mirunty! Mirunty, did you see?' squeals my nephew.

'What, Raja?' I bend my head to look out of the window at his angle to try and see . . . 'What is it?' I can see nothing particularly different or unusual in the sea of people, the boxlike shops, the hoardings, the painted slogans, the misty skyline.

'Ohhh! It's gone now! You didn't see! That . . . that tower?'

'No, I didn't. But you can point it out to me on the way back.'

'It was also built for the Asian Games, Mirunty!' my niece informs me.

'Mira-unty? Did you see the Asian Games?' chirps my nephew.

'No, Raja. Of course I didn't. How could I? I wasn't here.'

'But I don't mean here. I mean there.'

'Where?'

'In London.'

'In London? How could I see it in London?'

'On the television in London. It must have come on the news . . .'

The television in London! I laugh, highly amused at the idea of hearing a report on the Asian Games broadcast on the nine or ten o'clock news!

'I don't think the Asian Games came on the television in London, you know.'

'Do you have a TV?' interrupts my cousin-sister, her tone imperious.

'Yes I do.'

'And do you watch it much?'

'Well, no, I don't watch it that much. But I do quite often watch the news and I can tell you it has to be something pretty big – like a calamity or a major event – happening in India, for it to be on the TV in England!' I say with great assurance.

'Well!' returns Savitri, with equal assurance. 'I can tell you that the Asian Games was a pretty major event! All the countries in Asia were represented and came to Delhi! Just think of it! Some x number of countries representing some y number of people and totalling pretty well most of the world's population! I'd say it was a major enough event by any stretch of the imagination!' I note a definite irritation in her gear change.

'Oh, I agree with you completely!' I reply, responding to this opportunity of both explaining my point and illuminating the feelings of alienation and isolation of my life abroad. 'It certainly is a major event, and that's the whole point. But you see, over there they're very Eurocentric, and that means that in relation to the rest of the world – '

'I don't know about your sentrix or other tricks,' interrupts Savitri, asserting flatly, 'it must have been reported, and you just missed it!'

It dawns on me that her intention is to stick to her ground by re-establishing the hierarchy – that requires me to address her with the deference expected from the younger members of her husband's family. To test out my reading, I reply in a suitably chastised tone: 'Yes, Bhabiji, it could be.'

'Of course,' she returns unequivocally. Her self-assured profile looks gratified. She lunges into the slow lane to overtake a car with hardly a glance in the mirror. The bus whose path we have crossed hoots, as does my cousin-sister, the car we have overtaken, and everyone else around who has a hooter . . .

I look up at the sky and ask it absently if 'Eurocentric' exists in the Oxford dictionary? And what if it doesn't? Maybe that makes it a Eurotrick! . . . Any old tricks indeed! Eurotricks, Indotricks, yes, Indotricks! And what might they be? . . .

The car rears to a halt. A traffic light. I am jolted forward, and back – into the many Indias coming to a head-on, on-top-of-each-other stop, and presenting in their medley an image of seemingly undifferentiated chaos, confusion of possibilities . . . all shrouded and linked together by the eternal and omnipresent dust . . . Yes indeed! Everything here really does appear to linger and co-exist with everything else . . . sports cars alongside bullock carts wait for the light to change. New forms appear, old ones live on, as feudalism,

89

tribalism, capitalism merge or jog alongside . . . as indeed do Hinduism, Buddhism, Sikhism, Jainism, Judaism, Islam, Christianity, Zoroastrianism . . . and how many more? . . .

Savitri smiles at me, reassured – order has been re-established, and I have relearned the forgotten rule: that one does not contradict elders, whatever they say and even though the difference may only be two, three or four years! She turns around to tell the children to stop arguing, adjusts her cushions and then, finally, surveys the lower orders of traffic with the typical expression of members of her class: chin up, pout out, and an unseeing look as though the world were transparent. The dust hangs around suspended, watching . . .

'I suppose you've been going round seeing the family.'

'Trying to. But they're not all easy to get hold of! Look at Ravibhai!'

'Hmm,' she nods, looking absently through a dust-coated young girl who has approached our car, holding out a paper for us to buy as she simultaneously grapples to get to grips with a shawl, a small baby hitched on her hip, and a pile of newspapers.

'Well you'll see them all at the wedding.' The car rears to go almost knocking over the girl who desperately grabs my coin as she tries unsuccessfully to give me a paper and is left standing in the middle of the road as, around her, the manifold complexity of traffic blasts through the lights – each with its own determined direction and chosen pace.

The Italian-ice-cream hotel is situated on a large, and still developing site. In the winter dryness, surrounded by dust and rubble, it appears from the distance like a desert landscape, thrusting out of its entrails this eyesore of self-assertion in concrete and glass. As we approach, the desert image is further enhanced by the slow, sad files of desert people, who form the army of labourers who have built up Delhi with their sweat and blood. Their picturesque and colourful clothes in sharp contrast to the stark, unrelenting grind of their harsh working lives. I have seen them, and noticed them, throughout my childhood, on my visits back, as they built brick by brick the many mansions of the many aunts, uncles and cousins.

'Can't you put up a shelter for the children to play?' I had once asked, seeing babies grovelling in the dust attended to by six- and seven-year-olds. It was during the punishing June heat; I was ten at the time and being taken for the evening swim-and-chips-and-tomato-sauce at the club.

'What? What children? Them? Oh, they're used to it! Don't you worry about them!' In the car I had swallowed my salt tears, which they had attributed to the heat. What other reason could I possibly have for no longer wanting to go to the club!

'When I went off to school, Mirunty, there was nothing here, and when I came back, it was all here and all high, like magic!' chirps my nephew waving his arms about animatedly.

'What was?' I ask, suddenly aware that we have climbed the hill leading to the hotel and the car is being parked.

'This hotel! It was built so quickly you know!'

'Hardly magic, though, Raja,' I reply. 'Lots of hard labour you mean.' But Raja is only half listening as he skips along with his sister Rekha.

Inside, the hotel fulfils its promise of ostentation and impersonality – all marble, glass, leather and steel – and the patrons all swagger and sneer. Our table looks out over the vistas of Delhi, as well as the building works and the slow silent lines of men and women fetching, carrying, unloading and fetching all over again. How much you see depends on how you sit . . . on how far back in the chair, so that you can either see or overlook what you are overlooking . . . !

Savitri, who has quite forgiven me my earlier transgression, and appears to take my silence for deference, is now all solicitude, treating me like one of the younger members of the family.

'I'll just have a coffee, Bhabiji.'

'No, no, no, darling. I insist that you have something.

91

Come on, take what you like. Find something!' She hands me the menu.

'Well, maybe if they have rasgullas.'

'Rasgullas are best in Bengali market,' chips in my nephew. 'Aren't they, Mama? Aren't rasgullas best in Bengali market? Mama, why don't we get Meera aunty some rasgullas from Bengali market? Mama – ?'

'What? Stop pulling at my sari like that. Behave yourself, and what is it?'

'Meera aunty likes rasgullas, can we get her some from Bengali market please, Mama?'

'Yes, yes, of course. But what will you have now, Meera.'

'I'd really just like a coffee, Bhabiji.'

'Sure you won't have anything else?'

'Sure.'

'Not even a little cassata?'

'No. I'll wait for the rasgullas.'

The children wiggle and coo as we wait. Savitri looks around the room just in case there is a 'who' or a 'did you see' . . . My gaze involuntarily returns to the building site.

'You see, children, there? Those labourers? They are the real builders of your hotel, the makers of your magic, as you called it. Just lots of hard labour. Without them, there wouldn't be any hotel.'

'My God, Meera, you're just now speaking like one of these simplistic visitors! "Without them there wouldn't be . . . " indeed!' Turning to the children she corrects, 'They aren't the builders, they just carry out the work. Fetch and carry. If they didn't do it, donkeys would do it . . . or machines would do it . . . and I'm not saying that they are donkeys either, just that they are very grateful to have the work to do and to get a square meal a day.' The last is addressed to me, and though I am not expected to reply, I am spared the heavy silence by the timely arrival of the waiter.

As I lean forward to sip my coffee, the corner of my eye catches again and again the same movement . . . up . . . and down . . . relentlessly, helplessly . . . But no! That's me! Yes me that feels the helplessness sitting here, in this . . . this false, impersonal, inane, inhumane place . . . exuding greed and alienation . . . living so far away that even what I feel and say loses its very meaning. Speaking like a visitor! With the coffee I gulp down my feelings – of my own indignation, frustration, helplessness . . .

Savitri parks the car in the road, in double file, where it suits her. As the other traffic hoots around her, she shuffles in her glove compartment, takes out a pair of dark glasses, dusts them on the edge of her sari and puts them on.

'All right, if you stay with the kids, Meera, I won't be long!' She strides through the obstacles of traffic and people and into a teahouse. My nephew and niece chirp out their whispered argument and the odd bazaar beggar approaches the car. By the time Savitri returns three or more have gathered around for their coins; on seeing her they shuffle away quickly.

'Here, Meera.' She hands me a disposable earthen pot, sealed at the top with plastic and an elastic band. 'Rasgullas!'

'Thank you, Bhabiji.'

'And here, this is for you guys.'

'Oooh! Thank you, Mama . . . What are they? Are they laddus?'

'Don't open them in the car. Laddus!' She props up her cushions and settles into the driving seat. 'Silly kids! You're soon going to be drowning in wedding laddus, so why would I get you laddus? It's sandesh.'

'Daddy's favourite.'

'Yes, your Ravibhai loves sandesh.' She smiles at me, and then, hand on the hooter, blasts into the traffic.

On our return Bibiji is back in her position in the drawing room, chatting with the last two visitors – that there have been more is indicated by the positioning of the chairs pulled towards the fan heater blowing out warm air. Following the greetings, we all sit down, the children shyly responding to the neighbours' usual questions about school and holidays while Savitri tells Bibiji of the afternoon's menu. A very large box of laddus catches our eyes simultaneously.

'Wedding sweets?' asks Savitri.

'Yes, they arrived this afternoon. Will the children like some?'

'No, Aunty, they've had too much! And there will probably be some at home! Imagine those kids wanted me to buy them laddus! Laddus when there are so many family weddings on!'

'We hear that the bride's parents are putting on a very big show and that they've hired the Ashoka hotel . . . ' Mrs Rai throws in this information hoping it will be picked up and elaborated upon. For some reason, Bibiji is intent on curbing it.

'Only two halls have been booked and there will probably be two, three or four weddings going on in the other halls at the same time.' Bibiji's curt reply manages to arrest further discussion.

'Rani!' says my great-aunt when the visitors have left. 'Get me six paper bags from the top right-hand drawer of the sideboard.' Her voice is grave. 'I keep these brown bags because they always come in useful,' she explains as I hand them to her. She removes the cover from the large ornate box of laddus and starts to drop some into the first of the paper bags.

'It's a pretty huge box,' I say.

She nods her head thoughtfully, 'Yes, yes. Pretty huge! Huge show! That's what weddings have become today! Huge shows!' She hands me the first filled paper bag, saying, 'Here, this is for Chandu,' and starts to fill another one. 'In the old days we used to have langars!'

'What were they?'

'At a langar you distribute free food. We always distribute food, sweets, gifts to mark any auspicious occasion, and so before weddings, we would set up a langar and cook and distribute food to all. Anyone could come, without distinction, and anyone could eat.' She hands me the next bag of laddus.

'None of this rich giving to the rich only,' she explains, filling the next bag. 'Sometimes kitchens were set up for a week, a month or even a day. That didn't matter, the important thing was that this was Braham Bhoj – Braham after Brahman, the Supreme Being, and Bhoj, meaning food – and Braham Bhoj meant that you were feeding God through feeding God's creatures – because you fed the birds and animals too – and the needy. So you see, setting up a langar was also setting up an example, where the rich would serve and the poor would eat. But now it's all a show-off show, of about how rich they are, and how much they can afford to waste. And those who can't afford it are forced to do the same! All show! Huge show!'

I now have six laddu-laden bags in my lap, laden also with memories and feelings I think as I get up to place them on the table, gently so that they don't crumble.

'Nowadays they'll spend one lakh or more to hire a tent and elephants and chandeliers, throw away good food and drown themselves in drink and the more waste the more jolly good show it will be!'

'But tell me, Bibiji,' I say returning, 'I didn't know about langars which I think are wonderful, but what about dowries! Mama used to tell me about how the dowries would be displayed and people would come and see how much had been given. Wasn't that show?'

'Na, na, na, na, na!' Bibiji has assumed both the posture and voice of militant indignation. 'That was not show, or if some people used it like that it was certainly not what it was supposed to be! The displaying of the dowry was meant to protect the woman! You see, under the old law – but all that's changed now – the daughters did not inherit the property, so as their share of the wealth they received money, jewels, clothes in the form of a dowry which was their personal property and not to be touched by anyone. So, the dowries were displayed so that there were plenty of witnesses to what the girl had. In the old days, and in the original tradition, a dowry was a woman's protection, and now, today, it has become a woman's scourge!' Bibiji shakes her head and then relaxes back into her chair thoughtfully while I wait attentive, fascinated, for more. Suddenly, she reaches out for her book and pen.

'Yes. Well, change is always there,' she mutters, 'but the meanings have got lost and no one remembers.' Her voice is deep and rasping, her writing faltering.

Something hangs unsaid. I wonder what and I wonder why Bibiji changed her mind when she appeared to be so well launched in her reminiscences. What did she remember . . . reasons for her own not getting married? Was it to do with dowry maybe? And what is the story? And why doesn't anybody know, or ask it ? . . .

But as I watch her hand writing, slow and faltering – trying to contain . . . trying to regain her calm – I am quite decided that I too will not ask – for I am moved by a deeper feeling than curiosity. I listen to the sound of the pen on the paper and the rhythm re-establishing itself. Bibiji raises her head. We smile at each other.

'Rani. Distribute the sweets will you. Chandu, Maie, the sweeper, the dhobi, the mochi and the mali.

'And Minoo?'

'I've given to her family. That's how it's done. And then you can call for dinner when you want to. There's only us tonight. Daya's at Pushpa's till tomorrow. I think I might sleep early tonight.'

Nineteen

Bibiji is in her puja room, peforming the daily ritual she has done all her life since childhood. The room was incorporated into the very first drawings of the house, and according to Bibiji's instructions, designed small and contained but able to open out into the larger adjoining rooms on either side and thereby form a central altar for the more seasonal prayer gatherings attended by family and guests.

But this morning the room is enclosed except for the one door which is left ajar and through which I can observe her. But even if I couldn't I would be able to guess the familiar routine long observed and well remembered. The room itself is an accumulation of memorabilia. On the bits of wall without doors and window hang old photos of her deceased family, parents, sisters, brothers, including my grandfather, of gods and goddesses, saints and sages, and some unknown faces. In the centre is a large stool on which Bibiji sits in front of a low, rectangular table holding all the puja paraphernalia and above which are three shelves lined with the brass murthis of the many gods and goddesses in their manifold incarnations. Flanking her side, on another low table, are the books: the Ramayana, the Gita, the Veda . . . and the Guru Granth Sahib on its own stand, covered with an embroidered cloth. Next to these are two ugly, blistered and beat-up army jerry cans.

Everything is accessible at a stretch from her stool and needs to be so, for this morning, like every other morning, each of the brass figures will be taken down from its place,

97

bathed, wiped dry and then returned . . . row after row of all three rows. Then each of the deities will have a single flower placed in front of it, starting with Ganesh in the top right-hand corner and ending with the marble cosmic egg. After the offering of each flower, Bibiji will join her hands in reverent salutation before offering the next. Following the gods, each of the books will receive a flower and a salutation, as indeed will the two jerry cans – for they contain the precious Ganges water used for bathing the gods, but which is also holy in itself! Finally when all this has been meticulously done, Bibiji will light the incense and pray.

Bibiji is absently aware that I am watching her, but in India, private spaces are often mental spaces, and as long as I watch contained within myself and am not projecting a mental question, there will be no intrusion, no interruption, and our respective privacies will be maintained. With this observation, I leave the room, formulating under my breath the prayer I know Bibiji will recite, 108 times before she will rise from her seat . . .

> *Om bhur bhuva swaha*
> *Tat savitur varenium*
> *Bhargo devasya dhimahi*
> *Diyoyona prachodayatha.*

'Today what's your programme?' says Bibiji, joining me in the garden.

'Nothing till late afternoon. Sita's invited me to tea.'

'That's good. Then we can sit together and see what will happen this day.' Her eyes twinkle. 'Something will . . . something always does.' She eases herself into her chair.

'And if it doesn't, you can tell me a story!'

'That's right,' she agrees, neatly arranging the folds of her sari before collecting her book and starting once more to write her usual . . . ram, ram, ram. I lean over to see the date. It's still 1958.

'What do you do with the books when they're full?'

98

'Nothing.'

'Can I have the one you're writing in when it's finished?'

'What will you do with it?'

'Nothing. I just like it.'

'You can have it, but it will take some time. There are lots of others.'

'I'd like that one. Keep it for me.'

'Shanta and Pushpa took some and had them put in the foundations of their house when the first pujas were done.'

'That's a nice idea!'

'Your mother also wanted – ' Bibiji starts and then stops herself, leaving her unfinished sentence suspended in the air – quite ironical really – the unfinished sentence about the unbuilt house which was part of the unlived dream of my parents' longed-for return . . .

'You know in Lahore . . . ' Bibiji's voice is firm and loud, in a tone meant to interrupt my thoughts. I look up at her and meet the powerful gaze of her pitch-black eyes. 'In Lahore . . . ' she says again and smiles.

'You mean in the old days in Old Lahore . . . ' I respond.

'Yes, yes, in the old days, in Old Lahore. We had such a big, big house that all the different family units had their own set of rooms and even though the families kept growing there always seemed to be room for everybody!'

She stops writing for a moment. 'Yes, it was very big! It was about forty cannals of land. Now I don't exactly remember that in acres but I suppose it would be around seven or eight acres, something like that . . . '

'But that's huge! How was it so huge?'

'Well, there was lots of land then. You see the old city of Lahore used to be surrounded by a wall in which there were four gates and everyone lived inside the city walls. Then, when the British came to the Punjab . . . '

'When was that?'

'Oh, that's around the middle of the last century, 1850 or so. And when they came, they started to build their cantonments, and administration buildings and bungalows outside the walls of the old city. And, of course, they needed a big staff, and not only as jawans, clerks and orderlies, but educated people to be in the judiciary, the army, the civil service, things like that. And later on, these people also gradually moved out of the city, beyond the Shalimar Gardens, and started to build themselves nice big bungalows. We had two tennis courts, three servants' quarters, lawns, gardens, a well and near the well there was a peepul tree which even outsiders would come in to worship.'

'I remember Mama telling me about that . . . '

'And in our family, there was also this system – and in this system each working member of the family agreed to put ten per cent of their income into a family fund. This was so that any other member of the family in need could be properly looked after. For many years this custom was kept up.'

'Then what happened to it?'

'Oh, it gradually got dropped. In the beginning it worked and even the young men in the services posted all over the country would send their contribution. But then, after Bapuji died, some stopped and finally after Partition, when the old family homes were lost, the families broke into smaller units of their own and then it just stayed that way. But in Bapuji's day we were a big joint family, with one big home for everyone!'

'So all that ended with the Partition?'

'Yes, all that ended with the Partition.'

'So the glorious time was "after the British" and "before the Partition"?'

'That's the time I remember! And yes, they were good times.'

'So British rule was good then?'

'Well, I don't know about good . . . or bad. In the beginning they brought peace to the Punjab. They were good at fighting and law and order, but they never understood us, and then how long could we remain gulaams in our own land?'

We are interrupted as a small group of cows ambles

100

through the colony, nothing particularly unusual until one of them detaches herself, tempted by the row of seedlings in Bibiji's flower beds near the entrance gate.

'Hut, hut!' exclaims Bibiji, flapping her shawl and rapping her stick on her two-tiered table. 'Minoo Minoo! Where's Minoo? Chandu! Maie! Someone shoo the cow away.'

As I get up to do so, Minoo comes tearing down the drive brandishing a thin stick with the help of which she soon persuades the young animal to join her friends. Mrs Rai who appears on her way to visit, helps with a small pat-push.

'They're going to K.23, Biji,' calls out Minoo, nonchalantly beating the dust with her stick at the same time. 'I recognised her. It's Mrs Verma's cow and she's started taking her friends there now!' Minoo looks impudent.

'Forget about whose cow it is and come and help me pick up all these things,' says Bibiji, clearly ruffled.

'Are you all right, Mataji?' greets Mrs Rai, crossing the lawn towards us.

'But isn't this Mrs Verma's cow the one Aunt Daya was on about the other day?' I ask as, along with Minoo, I help collect Bibiji's belongings.

'Cows, cows!' grumbles Bibiji. 'See if you can find my pen, and where's my mala?'

Her papers once again in order, her sari tidied and her shawl re-arranged, Bibiji fingers her mala, trying to re-establish her calm as Mrs Rai takes her seat.

'Mrs Verma's brought her cow from Brindaban.'

'And she feeds it sweet chapatis. The servants told me . . .'

'Run along, Minoo, with your servant talk,' Bibiji says roughly, quickening her beading of the mala and closing her eyes to signify that she is not as yet ready to converse.

'What's all this about Mrs Verma's cow?' I ask Mrs Rai, but as she starts to tell me two more visitors make their way towards us. Not until much later, and following many other digressions, do I glean the necessary information about the cow.

Mrs Verma, a local resident and well-to-do widow, had for

some years been living in semi-religious retreat near one of the ashrams in Brindaban, where Lord Krishna used to graze his cows. Although Mrs Verma was kind to all the cows, during her time there she had adopted one particular cow as a pet. So that when her only son was transferred back to Delhi, and keen that his elderly mother should come and live with them or at least spend longer periods of time with them, she was naturally keen to bring her pet. This didn't appear to pose a problem as the Vermas had a very big garden having built their house on a bigger than double plot of land. So Nandini, that was the name Mrs Verma had given her pet, stayed there for a while until the municipality stepped in, imposing all sorts of restrictions and demanding all sorts of conditions to be fulfilled, like a cow house and a cow toilet and what not else. So, while these preconditions were being looked into, Nandini was being fostered by a local cowherd and would come every day to visit, play and spend the day.

'To think that in Hindu India we should not be able to keep a cow!' grumbles a neighbour.

'But it's not Hindu India, we're a secular state, Aunty,' replies her niece. 'In any case it's got nothing to do with Hindu, it's got to do with sanitation.'

'What sanitation? People keep dogs everywhere! And they're filthy animals.'

'No, no. Dogs are very sweet.'

'It's a modern, Westernised idea. Nobody kept dogs before the British.'

'The British' and 'The Partition'. Before . . . during . . . and after . . . for they are what still form living memory and will soon be forgotten.

A car comes and stops outside. Bibiji looks over her spectacles to see.

'Ah ha,' she smiles. 'The girls have come.'

We all turn to watch as the girls – Pushpa, Daya and another silver-haired aunt, Shanta – alight from the car and chat their way through the gate. On seeing the company, Aunt Pushpa detaches herself from her sisters and strides

102

ahead towards us and following the mandatory greetings and niceties she proceeds, characteristically, to announce the manifold activities she has been engaged in over the past few days – the complexity of her transactions, the value placed on her opinion, and the conflicting demands she has to respond to. Her sisters beam at her with pride, the others display admiration, while Bibiji just writes on . . .

As my three aunts sit down, I am struck at how different they are, almost as though they represent three completely different ways of being and confronting the world. Aunt Shanta, shy and quiet, withdraws into her chair as though wishing to disappear. Aunt Daya sits on its edge, alert and wide eyed, ready to respond, rear up and go. Aunt Pushpa bestrides her chair as though it were a chariot, energetically tossing her head and darting her eyes and brandishing her knitting needles so fast that they appear like Lord Vishnu's swirling discus, and tugging at her wool as though commandeering a horse. I am reminded of the story of the Great Goddess Durga who, invested with all the separate powers of the gods, had to perform the daunting task of destroying the demon Mahisha who was quick as lightning, could change his shape into anything and from whose every drop of blood which touched the earth a new demon formed. But Durga, the Undaunted One, commandeered her eighteen arms, elongated her tongue, and wielding her weapons, chopped up the demon, lapped up the blood and rode off on her tiger, laughing, triumphant, radiant. My mother would gesticulate all the movements when she told me this story . . .

'Well, Meera! You haven't been to see me, eh? Why? Too busy to spend time with the old aunts?' Aunt Pushpa laughs.

'I've tried to phone you many times . . . '

'But why phone me? Just come and see me.'

'But when I phone you're out . . . '

'But then I come back in. The house is always open. You can come when you like, do what you want, order something to eat.'

'Yes, of course, I'd forgotten that houses are always

open . . . '

'You've been away too long. Either you must come here for much longer or you must come here more often.' Like a storyteller she turns to her audience for participation; they all nod their heads. 'See, see, everybody agrees.'

'She doesn't just stay away out of choice,' comes Bibiji's voice. 'Why make the child feel bad. She's only here for a little time; what's the point of her going in and out of your house ordering this and that and waiting for you when you yourself have told us you have so much to do that you're never in?'

Aunt Pushpa effuses – clarifications, justifications, explanations – and by the end of it all I am to go for lunch the next day at one.

'Oh-ho,' she suddenly remembers. 'Tomorrow is a Tuesday. It's my fast. I don't cook any meat or eggs! I know what, I'll take you to the Hanuman Mandir.'

'No, Aunty, I'll come for lunch. I'm not much of a meat eater and Sita is taking me to the Hanuman Mandir. I'm having tea with her and Sanjay and tomorrow morning she's taking me to the mandir.'

'See! What did I tell you! No time for the old aunts!'

I am rescued from having to reply by Chandu coming out to ask if he should set out the lunch.

Twenty

'I say, poor you!' says my cousin Sita as we drive off. 'Stuck up all day with all the old ladies of the colony!'

'I don't mind. In fact I quite like it.' It occurs to me as I say it, that I do. 'I listen to the stories of the old days, and also, old age has a different feel here.'

'The old days, huh! Doesn't take much to get them talking about that!'

'No, it doesn't! But that's okay by me because I love to listen and I feel I don't know nearly enough.'

Sita smiles. 'You don't mind a bit of a drive do you. I have to pick up something on the way.'

'No, no. Not at all. I love driving in the car.'

Sita, I note, drives more slowly and gently than Savitri. Sita and Savitri! The two paragons of Indian womanhood! Ideal wives – dutiful, devoted, deferential. I always preferred Savitri who was so spirited and clever that she even outwitted Yama, the god of death! But from the two in the family, I prefer my cousin Sita.

'What are you thinking about?'

'Stories! About Sita, and Savitri. The great ideals!'

'Don't forget Sati! So the old ladies are fogging up your head with their tales, eh?' She laughs. 'In any case I'm glad you're okay there; I've been feeling really bad that I haven't managed to find the time to spend with you until now.'

'Don't worry. I know all about it. It's the season! Usha told me.'

'The what?'

'The season – for socialising, shopping and parties.'

Sita laughs. 'The season for hard work as far as I'm concerned! Sanjay's niece got married. That's his eldest sister's daughter, but you can imagine what that meant for us! He's the only maternal uncle and everything was left to who? – yours truly! But it's over now! And I can spend the whole day with you tomorrow if you like!'

'I have to lunch with Aunt Pushpa tomorrow. She wants you to come as well.'

'I hope you didn't say I was free all day?'

'No, I didn't say anything.'

'Good. No, I won't come. Aunt P. is always here and I make my round of family calls regularly. I'll do some of my other errands so I can make some time and see you again.'

'That's nice of you Sita. Thanks.'

' "Thanks", she says. You're not supposed to thank me! You're supposed to expect it as of right! That's what families are supposed to be about, silly!'

Our drive through the city is like a drive past the many moments in the capital's history – Hindu temples, Mogul monuments, Lutyens' layout, and the edifices of modern India – for Delhi has been built and forgotten and found and rebuilt and redesigned for so many hundreds, no, thousands of years. 'The many change and pass . . . earth's shadows fly' . . . leaving behind their monuments, their stories, and their dust . . .

'By the way. Watch a bit what you say to Aunt Pushpa. See that you tell her just what you want to tell her. She has a way of asking questions and squeezing information out – you have to learn to dodge your way around.'

'How do I do that?'

'Oh, it's simple, you just smile. You don't say yes, you don't say no, you give vague answers if you have to, you laugh frequently and you try to change the topic of conversation. A good way is usually by giving praise, at least I find it works!'

'You sound like an expert!'

'You have to be. Otherwise the strangest stories spread around.'

'Yes, I know. I remember what it's like.'

'I mean, look, I haven't met you until now and yet I've been informed.' She smiles.

'Tell me.'

'Meera's in town, did you know? You mean she hasn't called you yet? Oh-ho I thought you'd be the first person she'd get in touch with. She's come on her own you know . . . hasn't even brought Maya! By the way Meera, that reminds me, I hope you've at least brought a picture of my niece!'

'I'll have a look. I might have one with me.'

'I'd like to send her something, I don't know what, but the picture will inspire me.'

'But carry on. Tell me what else you've heard. I'm flattered that anyone should bother.'

'They don't really bother, they just idly chat. But why don't you tell me what you'd like me to know.'

'I will. But you tell me more first.'

'Nothing much more, except that you've been sending parcels to Renu in Calcutta and that you like it here and would like to come back. What did you send to Renu?'

'I didn't. It was a friend's parcel.'

'Ah well! You see what I mean then. And you want to come back?'

'Well, yes, but it does seem very complicated . . . a place to live, earning a living, a school for Maya . . . '

'Talk to Sanjay. He might have some ideas. He's good at helping one to think straight . . . playing devil's advocate. He enjoys that. I always tell him he became a lawyer because he likes to argue!'

Sita's home is a shining example of good housekeeping, tastefully decorated and well maintained. My cousin-brother, Sanjay, recently returned from a game of squash, looks spruced up and trim. As we enter he is helping himself

107

to a small peg before tea.

'Will you have some? Or do you not drink till after dusk like your cousin?' He laughs, anticipating my refusal. 'So. How are you enjoying your visit?'

Visit! Visitor! You're talking like a visitor, Savitri had said. But it is a visit.

'Meera's thinking of coming back to India!' announces Sita.

'Really? What, with the whole family? Or are you one of these modern women who think they should make their lives independently!' He emphasises the last word and laughs.

'Don't be silly now, Sanjay.'

'I'm really just exploring the idea at the moment.'

'I see! So what do you want to come back to?'

'Well . . . to India!'

'Yes, but what does India mean to you?'

'What? India mean to me?'

'That's right! What is it you want to come back to.'

Sita smiles and pours the tea. I had been forewarned of his cross-examining tone – but the question sets me thinking . . . feeling. What does India mean to me? What is India? India is people . . . human warmth. India is time . . . and sun and smiling faces. India is dreams, memories, stories, and dust. And India is a place where there is so much that needs to be done . . . yes . . . 'and each one of us has a duty to help rebuild and heal our country'. My left hand tingles with a memory, involuntarily I rub it as I recollect . . .

'What is it then?' Sanjay interrupts.

'What? Oh! I suppose it's . . . people . . . and sun . . . and belonging . . . and meaning.'

Sanjay laughs. 'Yes! All very poetic and idealised! Don't want to sound harsh, but that's what happens to expatriates! Distance idealises!'

'Well, I don't enjoy my expatriate reality. I feel a misfit, misunderstood, misinterpreted – stereotyped with no existence as an individual. I don't know, it's difficult to explain.'

'Yes, I'm sure it is, but at the same time, I think that some of your illusions need dispelling. I'm sure you speak from your heart, but I'm going to speak to your head. You get my meaning?' Having finished his drink, he picks up a cup of tea. 'Now as far as being an individual is concerned, you can forget about that idea here. We don't even have such a concept. Life is just a round of family duties and obligations for most people, and individuals,' he emphasises the word, 'individuals are only for a few of the very rich, and only a few of them, too, mind you. As for being misinterpreted – ha! Let me tell you, we have great expertise in that. Gossip and idle chatter are the order of the day and stories grow quicker and wider than the banyan tree. You know the banyan tree whose branches drop down to the ground, take root and in turn give more branches . . . '

' . . . which again fall to the ground and take root.' interrupts Sita.

'Yes that's right. Sita knows what I mean.'

'We all know about banyan trees,' laughs Sita.

'And gossip,' adds Sanjay as we all laugh. 'And the family!' continues Sanjay. 'Yes, yes indeed, the family! Woe to the one who says anything against the wonderful family you can always count upon for – nothing. For anything that they do for you is never forgotten, and has to be repaid twenty times over, and you're still in debt.' He turns to his wife for affirmation, who demonstrates her noncommittal 'don't say yes, don't say no' laugh, and then shakes her head at me to say it's not true.

'Aha! My dear wife does not agree. But it's to her peril. She's one of these family-minded people always doing things for everyone, but the day she needs them – I'd like to see who will be around!'

'You will!' returns Sita quite disarmingly.

'Sucker Sanjay! Ah yes, sucker Sanjay will be there all right!' Sanjay leans back into the sofa clearly enjoying the topic. 'The family, talk about blood – about one being their blood – and that is significant. For what it means is that your blood – belongs to them. It's not your blood, it's their blood – and everything must be repaid in blood!'

'Come on, Sanjay, you're getting carried away. You're just confusing Meera and voicing your resentments.'

'I'm not confusing Meera. I'm sure she understands me. Don't you Meera?'

'From my heart or from my head?' I try to laugh lightly.

'Now most of the family is in Delhi . . . '

'And Chandigarh, and Simla . . . '

'Okay, okay, Chandigarh and Simla, but mostly in Delhi, and the point I'm trying to make is that Delhi is not India. It's just Delhi. A government city. A city of sycophants, yes, men, chamchas. The value of a man is measured by who he knows, what strings he can pull, what favours he can grant. Personal worth? Forget it, yar! And if you're searching for meaning and belonging – then it's the pits!'

'Sanjay!' Sita exclaims, and laughs to clear the air of her husband's bitter eloquence.

'And let me tell you something more. If you want to live in Delhi then the one thing you will need plenty of is money! Without it, you are nobody – and don't imagine you can get that kind of money from a salary.'

'Come on now, Sanjay. You're being of no help at all. Give Meera some practical ideas.'

'Practical ideas to make money in India? Ah, it's very simple. If you want to make money, you have to make yourself a niche in our new and fastest-growing industry of selling India! Export! Business! Export clothes! Export philosophy! Export culture! Export spirituality! Export tourism! Export nostalgia. Export the Raj, the festivals, the raw materials. At present India is an eminently saleable country and I suggest you find yourself a place in the boom business.' Sanjay laughs heartily. 'And while you think about what you can export and to whom, let me get you a drink – after all that I'm sure you could do with one. I certainly can.' Sanjay strides over to the drinks cabinet. 'What about you Seetu?' he asks gently.

110

'Okay. But a small one,' replies Sita.

'You know, it's difficult to come back to India once you have left it,' says Sanjay, handing us our drinks.

'But I never left – I got taken away.' I reply.

'Oh, Meera!' exclaims Sita, getting up from her place by the tea trolley to come and sit next to me on the sofa. 'Really Sanjay! Why do you have to be so heavy handed!'

'I think you underestimate Meera's intelligence, Sita. I'm only telling her a few home truths and playing the devil's advocate, like you keep telling everyone I do! "Don't mind my husband," she tells people, "he's a rough diamond. But a diamond none the less!" Eh, Seetu?'

'You remember that year you spent with us in Simla, Meera?' asks Sita, deliberately changing the subject.

I nod and smile at the memories. 'Very well.'

'It would have been so nice if you could have stayed on . . . '

But I was only a child at the time and had wanted to return to my own parents, however far away they lived . . .

'Meera and I understand each other.' Sanjay sips his drink. 'You know why? Because we're both poets at heart!'

'How did you know I wrote poetry?'

'I didn't,' he laughs. 'But it must have been your parents' aspiration when they named you after the great poet.'

My parents' aspiration for me? Again my left hand tingles . . .

'And mine called me Sita to be an ideal wife I suppose.' Sita pouts fetchingly.

'But that you are, my Seetu, that you are! You see, I too am a dreamer like you Meera – searching for kindred spirits and meaning and utopias over the horizon . . . and in the whisky.' He adds the last looking through his glass. 'That is why we need the likes of the Sitas and the Martins to earth us with their reality principle . . . '

Martin as a reality principle! I wrestle with the idea, and with the tinge of disloyalty, that I have thought so little about Martin during my visit so far . . .

111

'In India,' says Sanjay, 'there are those who eat . . . and those who get consumed . . . ' He downs his drink and looks thoughtfully at his glass as though considering his thoughts.

'Bas, Sanjay. Enough!' interrupts Sita. She turns to me like a gracious hostess. 'We haven't given Meera a chance to say anything – we don't even know about her situation . . . '

'Plenty of time for that. But she needs to know what to expect! Believe me I understand your aspirations, Meera! There's no place like India! It's the best place to live! But you have to be prepared to stay in the mould, not break from it . . . and this may mean . . . ' As Sanjay grapples with his thoughts to continue, Sita is clearly intent on steering the conversation in a different direction which she skilfully manages to do. I find myself absently replying to platitudes about plays in London, wondering what Sanjay was going to say and trying to contain the ever-flowing flood of memories.

'I really don't know what got into Sanjay that he went on like that and was so unhelpful,' says Sita as she drives me back.

'What did he mean about not breaking moulds?'

'Take no notice of all that. He just had too much. You see Sanjay's a really good and able man but not always very practical. He wants to *do* things . . . and in India you have to *be* someone first before you can do things.'

'I see.'

'We're all born into a family and certain situations. And the family will help. Of course they will. You should go and see them. See Uncle Gulu or Uncle Kishore or Ravibhai . . .'

'The elusive Ravibhai . . . '

'Yes, Ravibhai as well. Be specific. Ask straight out. Say you're looking for something, what can he suggest and who can he arrange for you to meet. If you want a job, tell him to help you find one. How did you get your present job in London?'

'It was advertised, I applied and went for an interview.'

'That was lucky. Well here it works by contacts!' Sita states matter of factly, 'You'll meet lots of people at the wedding.

Can't you stay longer?'

'It's difficult. Maya has to be back at school and I to work.'

'With your MA in English you can do better than library work here. You could teach at the university, but that's not very well paid – but you could easily get something in advertising. Ravibhai or Uncle Gulu could help you there. But the best thing will be if Martin can fix something from over there then you'll get an overseas salary and everything, that will be best.'

'I don't know yet what Martin wants to do.'

Sita throws me a quick look. 'My God, Meera, you're not thinking of coming on your own are you?' she exclaims. 'I mean, India is no place for a woman on her own. Surely you can't be contemplating . . . I mean, a woman's place is by her husband!'

'You really are a Sita!' I tease. 'There must be something in names after all – it's not for nothing yours is Sita!'

'What, so you imagine because you're called Meera you can just get up and go!'

'Did Meera do that?'

'Well. Not quite. But she did become a wandering songstress going from here to there.'

'Well, I'm not planning on doing anything quite like that. Like I said, I'm just exploring . . . and who knows? Nothing may come of it all.' The realisation of what I have just said feels like an icy wave through my body, leaving me stiff and brittle as I make my way from the car.

To my astonishment, Bibiji's drawing room is quite empty of visitors, though the signs that there have been some are clear. Sita leaves after a short greeting, announced as such when she enters the room.

'Burri Aunty this is a hello and goodbye at the same time. Must rush, Sanjay and I are expected at an official dinner . . . But I'll see you tomorrow when I come to fetch Meera.'

Bibiji sits in her great chair, writing, while Maie, squatting at her feet, is massaging them with oil. As Sita leaves and I sit down, Maie smiles and leans over to stroke my leg affectionately. Her eyes sparkle with a light as though she had never known sorrow – and yet she's had more, much more, than her fair share, for I remember being told she lost her whole family during the Partition. She herself was left for dead, but had survived with one small son. What horror, what agony! Maybe it was so great that it transformed into something else. Can that happen? Like boiling water transforming into steam and dissolving away?

'So?' asks Bibiji. 'How was it? How was the tea?'

'What?' I reply, tearing myself away from the gentle look in Maie's eyes and the tenderness in her toothless grin.

'Sita's tea? Sanjay was there?'

'Yes.'

'The children still away on the school holiday?'

'Yes.'

'And what did you young people talk about?'

'What everyone talks about. The state of the country! Export business! The politicians . . . nepotism . . . '

Bibiji nods her head knowingly. 'Yes, yes, it's true. People no longer enter public service to serve any more. Nowadays they do it for their own advancement, their own profit. It's become a disease and everyone is getting contaminated.'

'I must say I find it all increasingly confusing.'

'What exactly, my rani?'

'I don't know exactly. Everything! Sanjay asked me what I wanted to come back to . . . and went on to paint such a . . . picture. A few "home truths" as he called them. I don't know . . .' I shake my head and meet Bibiji's eyes – luminous black framed in the luminous white of her hair. Their look invites me to explore.

'You know what I think the trouble is, Bibiji? For me, India has got something to do with being a child. Something to do with feeling loved, protected and belonging. Maybe even something to do with my parents' own longing . . . longing to return. For the child in me it is warm and familiar, and for the grown up that I am, it is a strange land, in which I

114

don't know my way around.' Bibiji listens.

'But now, my parents are no more. The world of my childhood has gone and I can't seem to find what I am looking for.'

Bibiji nods her head in silence. 'Nah, rani,' she starts gently, her voice soothing, 'it doesn't just go. It stays and remains . . . but changed and different. Other things get grafted on, but India is all the things you feel it to be, and much else as well . . . '

'It's as though everything has moved on, I have got left behind and can't make any sense of anything.'

As always there are interruptions – one thing which doesn't change, I observe, as a group of shawl-clad ladies make their way up the drive. Bibiji follows the frown of my look and says gently, 'Ah yes. There is a meeting tonight of the Women's Welfare Committee. It was arranged a long time ago, rani. We'll talk again in the morning, accha!'

'I'm going off with Sita tomorrow morning.'

'Well, when you come back, in the evening. There'll be plenty of time, rani. Rest now. Forget about all this. Enjoy yourself tomorrow; don't cloud your mind, rani. It is not wholesome.'

Twenty-one

Dear friend,

I am getting increasingly confused. My search appears only to unfold layers of greater complexity as the clock time ticks and my stay approaches its end. I wish I could prolong it . . . find some way . . . I need more time . . .

This afternoon Sanjay asked what it was I wanted to return to and what did India mean to me. The question made me feel deeply vulnerable. I thought of my childhood . . . I missed my parents. I remembered our treasured visits to India, the feelings of warmth and belonging – the sense of purpose, the idealism – and it was all this I wanted to return to. But as I thought of it, another memory surged, another memory also connected to my childhood . . . my parents . . . India. I remembered it then, and even now I can feel the tingle in the palm of my left hand . . .

I must have been eleven or twelve years old. We were here for a longish stay, it was the holidays – full of childhood enchantment, of sun and laughter and play – I was skipping along with my cousins and friends clenching in my fists the precious coins of pocket money with which I was allowed to buy anything – even aam papad, the cheap leathery and sour kind which I was told was bad for the throat and no grown up would buy me. A beggar woman with a child accosted me. I stopped to give her one of my coins; as I did so she grabbed my wrist and twisted it painfully open and appropriated the whole of my treasure. As I was about to cry out through pain and indignation she started to shout that I was trying to take her money.

'Your parents will give you more. I have a child to feed,' she hissed at me before rushing off.

I'd held back my tears, shocked and confused. On returning to my room I cried and cried and cried and I washed my hands again and again, trying to wash away the pain, the touch, the memory, the injustice and the confusion of it all.

In the mansion where we were guests, I was summoned to lunch. I didn't go saying I had a stomach-ache. Papa came to see if I was all right and I told him through my tears what had happened, and how I wouldn't eat until someone gave me a good answer as to why there was so much poverty in India, and why there were people who had nothing to eat when there were others who had much too much.

The room was dark, the heavy drapes had been drawn to keep out the heat and glare of the April sun. My father's eyes appeared like little lights in the dark room as he sat down on my bed and in his most wonderful story-telling voice soothed and explained – what was it now he said? That different people would give me different answers to my question – often unsatisfactory and sometimes conflicting – but that my sense of outrage was quite right and that when I grew up I could transform it into action. That there was a lot of work which needed to be done in India . . . now that India was free – at last!

'And it is our duty to rebuild and heal the country, but you must wait till you are grown, and meanwhile prepare yourself, because, you see,' he continued, 'at each stage of our lives we have specific duties to fulfil and these we must do well, so that we can develop healthily in mind and body to assume our next lot of tasks. As you grow older you will make choices and then be responsible for those choices. But for now, while you are still a child you must do the duties expected of you as such – learn your lessons, listen to your elders, show respect to our hosts, and eat your lunch so that you can grow big and strong for all the work you will need to do when you are older. And keep the memory of this incident to remind you to always show respect and concern for all people. Because this will help you later for your work . . . '

The memory hurts. It feels like a knot in my chest – a constriction of so many feelings and emotions. The India I am encountering has switched off from the India I want to meet and to which I can't find the way, and I feel both that I have betrayed and . . . been betrayed.

I can't think any more. I'll stop writing for now.

Twenty-two

As we drive to the Hanuman Mandir, I am again flooded with images of memories – this time about the Great Hanumanji: from the epic, Ramayana, whose stories were among the many that enchanted my childhood, and all served to recall and strengthen the magical connection to India. It was a feeling which the exiled me would liken to being like the furthest branch of an immense old tree tossing in the wind, seemingly frail and forlorn, but secure in the knowledge of being connected to a greater strength with deep roots providing infinite nourishment. But Hanuman was a monkey, playful and accessible. He didn't pontificate and preach wise words – he just did things and expressed through his deeds all his qualities of strength, speed, power, dynamism and devotion. He leaped across oceans, uprooted mountains, soared through the skies, darted around like fire – and all this he could do because he was motivated by a greater power, the power of love – and when he opened his breast he revealed, enshrined in his heart, a picture of Sita and Rama . . . Ah yes! That's how the stories were told!

'What are you smiling about?' asks Sita.

'I was just thinking of Hanumanji and all the many stories and the many versions of the same story I have heard.'

'You and your stories, Meera!' Sita laughs. 'Do you remember the Hanuman Mandir near Simla?'

'Yes, that's right. Full of well-fed, cheeky monkeys.' We both laugh at our shared childhood memory. The Hanuman temple in Simla was on a hill, with steps leading up to the shrine itself. All around there were trees and everywhere, but everywhere, there were monkeys! Swinging from the branches, running up the steps, sitting on the rails, and playing in the sun on the temple roof. This was their place – and it was as if they knew that here they were gods, and behaved with a commendable measure of self-restraint. They wouldn't just snatch the bag of nuts from your hands, but wait politely until it was offered, which it invariably was – we always bought them for that purpose, monkey nuts. Maybe that's why they were called monkey nuts, because they were fed to the monkeys . . .

'There aren't so many of them now. I mean there are still lots but not as many as there were when we were children.'

'What happened?'

'I don't know. Maybe so many were sent to America that . . .'

'Oh, my God, yes! I remember now! The monkey planes!'

'That's right! Those plane loads and plane loads of monkeys that used to be sent off to American labs for experiments. And do you remember people who were willing to accompany the monkey planes could get free rides.'

'Poor monkeys! I remember that, and how upset we used to get. Yes, I remember it all now, but I'd completely forgotten. I thought I remembered most things of the eight months I spent with you all in Simla.'

Export business, I reflect. 'Why did they allow such things to happen. And who allowed it?'

'God knows! Though if Sanjay were here, he'd surely deliver you a passionate exposé. All I can say is thank God it's stopped. It was disgusting and cruel.'

Only God knows . . . and thank God for stopping it. 'It's funny, in the West they think of us as peace-loving, pacifist and vegetarian.'

'Well, we're all that as well, aren't we?' Sita smiles while I nod my head and think about it all: export, Simla, monkeys, Hanuman . . . I close my eyes to see what else will emerge from the memory store.

'Good heavens!' I exclaim. 'I just remembered something else!'

'What's happened?'

'Memory's a funny thing. I closed my eyes to think of Hanuman and wondered what image of him would emerge . . . '

'I always think of the one of him uprooting the mountain and bringing the whole thing along because he couldn't remember the name of the herb he'd been sent to find on it.' She laughs. 'The kids love that story too! Which one did you think of?'

'That's what's funny. The image that I saw was of a bronze statue they have of him at the Victoria and Albert Museum in London – and there's a whole incident connected with that.'

'Yes?'

'I'd forgotten about it until now. Martin and I had once stopped at the V and A, that's this museum in London . . . '

'Yes, I know the one.'

'In any case, there was this notice announcing a lunch-time talk on the Indian collection – and as we happened to be just in time we went in. And there was this man who talked about the collection, how and when it was acquired, and showed slides of paintings and miniatures and things. Then he told us how for a very long time the museum never purchased a single item of Hindu art.'

'Really?'

'Yes. Yes, apparently they couldn't appreciate or understand it and there'd been this man called Ruskin who'd written that there was nothing of interest or beauty or whatever in Hindu art, and so the first ever item of Hindu art that the museum obtained was in the form of a gift from William Morris – a man whom Martin greatly admires – and then he showed this slide of a beautiful South Indian bronze Hanuman standing doing namaste.'

'Did you go and have a look at the original after the lecture?'

'Yes, we did. It was really beautiful – and it was that image which came to my mind just now.'

Sita smiles me a reply, but the subtleties of this recollection are lost on her. And what does it really matter from here that one of them there rejected and the other admired. Sita never had to grow up explaining and justifying her Indian identity! We look around for a place to park, hooting our way through the crowd who don't take much notice anyway.

Tuesday is the day of Hanuman, it is the day of Mangal or Mars. It is a day when some shops are closed, and intoxicants, like alcohol and meat, are not sold. And around the precinct of the Hanuman temple in the city centre it is a day when there is a regular fair of stalls and sellers, and pedlars and beggars, frequented by strollers, shoppers and worshippers. And it is, of course, the most wonderful place to buy bangles – there are whole stalls of nothing but every conceivable bangle imaginable.

'You can only get better than this in Old Delhi,' Sita tells me. 'But then that's one heck of a trek!'

'Let's just stroll through the lot and then come back and buy,' I suggest.

We stroll past the many stalls selling nick-nacks, hair ornaments, costume jewellery, clothes, past palm readers, snake charmers, a group of young women drying their newly decorated, hennaed hands in the sun and watch briefly the skill with which the intricate patterns are worked. I love all this! I love all this, I say to myself, beaming out my smiles all around me – and so what, if it is this carefree world of fun, colour, and laughter of my childhood that I want to return to!

'Look!' says Sita pointing to the food stalls. 'Chaat! You want some?'

'Maybe later,' I reply looking at the chaat stalls ahead – the forbidden food of my childhood – my mouth waters. We weren't allowed it in the cold season, because it would give us a cold; we weren't allowed it in the hot season because it would upset our tummies; and we weren't allowed it during the rainy season, because it was the season of illnesses and so it would surely make us ill. As far as we were concerned, it was a conspiracy! As we get nearer to the temple itself, stalls selling sweets and flowers take over and we are among the crowds of devotees.

'Shall we go in?' I ask Sita.

'I'll wait for you here if you want to. But I won't go in,' replies Sita, her voice sounding almost petulant.

'Why? Do you just not like temples?'

'No, nothing like that! I'm just very angry with Hanuman-ji.' To my quizzical expression she replies, 'Oh, I've told him!'

'I see,' I return. 'Did you have a row?' I manage to swallow my laugh to listen to Sita who, with a most earnest face is remembering her annoyance with the god.

'Six months, six full months, I kept the fast, every Tuesday from dawn to sunset. Every week I came here, I prayed, I made my offerings, gave alms, did the pujas and everything. There was a good possibility that Sanjay could have become a judge – I mean it wasn't just a wild dream I was praying for – but what really upset me was that the news that he hadn't been appointed came on a Tuesday. That really took the cake! It was just too bad!'

'Was it before or after your . . . fas– ,' but my laughter drowns the end of my sentence.

'You can laugh, Meera. Sanjay's a good man and very capable.'

I throw my arms around my cousin, looking so radiant in her righteous indignation. 'I'm not laughing at you! Or your prayers! I'm just laughing at the . . . whole image . . . the whole idea! You know in the West people don't have rows with their gods – it's all reverence and awe, at least for those who still believe.'

'That's probably why there aren't many who do,' replies Sita matter of factly. 'Do you want to go in to the temple?'

'What, without you? No. I wouldn't know what to do!'

'Oh, it's very simple,' returns Sita. 'You just take one of

those trays and fill it with your offerings, go to those stalls, get some sweets, some flowers, an oil lamp and you can put some coins as well. Then you climb up to the temple, squeeze your way in – it's best just to allow yourself to be pushed along with the crowd going to the shrine. Once you're there you pay your homage, hand your tray to one of the priests – he'll take the offerings and give them to the god and return you some of the sweets – that's then the prasaad. Then you take that and squeeze back into the flow of those coming out of the temple, and that's it.'

'And that's it?'

'If the crowd is moving, which looks as though it is, you can be in and out in twenty minutes!'

I look at the steady flow of people making their way in and out of the temple . . .

'No!' I reply, returning my gaze to the stalls. 'I think I'll give it a miss. I'm not familiar with temples.'

'As you wish!'

We return to the bangles and baubles and trinkets, and Sita, having insisted that she wants these to be her presents to Maya, is quite carried away. By the end of it she has managed to fill four boxes.

'They're quite light!' she says, handing me half her load as we start to make our way towards the car.

'I really enjoyed that! I'd have loved to have a daughter for whom I could buy trinkets and things. When you come with Maya let me take her shopping . . . Oh, by the way, did you want some chaat?'

'No, no. I'll save myself for Aunt Pushpa's lunch. What about you?'

'It's my fast. I don't eat anything cooked till the evening.'

'But I thought you were angry –'

'Oh, but I still keep the fast. I just don't go and give offerings.'

'I see.'

'Aunty Sheela was trying to persuade me to keep the Saturday fast for Shanni, that's Saturn, and it's supposed to

124

be to remove obstacles. But I decided to stick to the Tuesdays.'

'In spite of your row,' I tease.

Sita laughs! 'Yes, in spite of my row, as you call it. You're really tickled about this row business, aren't you?'

'Don't mind me. It's just that . . . like I said . . . I can't imagine in the West that they have rows with their gods – it's mostly reverence and awe.'

'How boring! I'm told that Savitri's been keeping a Friday fast for Santoshi ma.'

I am surprised at the idea of Savitri fasting, or denying herself anything, but Sita clarifies my thoughts by informing me that this is a new goddess who is supposed to grant wishes.

'Santoshi ma has quite a cult following. I'm surprised that you haven't heard of her, but then of course she is fairly new!'

'Oh, I'm not really into gods and goddesses you know! Just stories!'

As we drive along to Aunt Pushpa's house I find myself wondering how many names of deities, and how many stories, I can remember.

'Have you any idea how many deities there are supposed to be?'

'In India?'

'Yes!'

'Do you mean actual different ones or different names for the same? I mean some of them have a thousand names.'

'I've got the figure 330 million in my head. But I don't quite know what –'

'No that sounds too much. Maybe 3, or 33 million. But then, in India, anything is possible . . . '

We swerve into the driveway and Sita parks her car behind Aunt Pushpa's. The maidservant comes out to tell us that everyone is out but expected any minute.

'I'll dash off then, Meera. You'll make my apologies, won't you?' And then turning to the maidservant Sita adds with urgency in her voice, 'Lakshmi, be sure to tell Aunt Pushpa that I came by to greet her. You'll remember to tell her won't you?'

Lakshmi shakes her head to signify that of course she will and that she understands the importance of the instruction.

'And Meera, you tell her the same,' she adds to me in English. 'One has to be alert to avoid misunderstandings in this family. And remember also what I told you the other day.'

'Don't say yes, don't say no, and when in doubt, laugh . . .'

'Absolutely correct!' Sita demonstrates the laugh as she drives off.

Twenty-three

As Aunt Pushpa is out, and the garden looks inviting, I stroll into it, still trying to distinguish the sound of Sita's car as it dissolves into the traffic. Lakshmi seems to have anticipated my movement and is already following me with a cane chair which she places in a gentle half shade of the tree – where the sun still flickers through the shadows of the moving leaves. I had intended to stroll around, but since the chair is there . . .

'Tea? Lemon water?' she asks as I sit down.

'Nothing. I'll just sit here and wait for the moment.'

'Accha!' Lakshmi shakes her head and smiles and watches me for a while before going off towards the house.

Sit and wait! Watch and listen! The sun, the sounds, the light, the heat, the smells – all seem to combine to create a special kind of . . . what is it? an effect? . . . a feeling? . . . a sensation? . . tactile almost – something which touches but cannot be grasped . . . cannot be understood. Maybe it belongs to a realm of experience beyond understanding and words . . . Is there something about India, I wonder, that invites this kind of speculation, or is speculation simply a response to confusion or ignorance? As I search for the word and half wonder about the meanings of words, a little bird comes hopping on the grass – a little bird whose name I do not know and can only describe as a pretty blue-green bird with a tuft upon its head. What would a name do? Make it prettier? Give it more life? It would differentiate it, mark its qualities, its specialness – and give it respect. What about my name? Meera! What does Meera mean? Me? What is Me and who am I? Who . . . am . . . I? To my surprise, the question overwhelms me with an intense feeling of restlessness, impelling me to get up from my chair and leave – to leave it all behind, the question, the feeling, the restlessness. I quickly make my way across the lawn into the house . . . and the question is blinded out by the blackness of the room after the glaring sunlight outside.

Slowly I compose myself, and Aunt Pushpa's room comes into focus, revealing all its well-known – and intensely familiar – features, for I have seen this room many times over the years. I have visited it in different cities and different houses, in the moutains and in the plains . . . I have seen this room dismantled, packed up, loaded on to a truck, 'transferred', 'sent off to a new posting'. And I have seen it again unpacked, and reconstituted with its same imposing glass chandelier, its chintz curtains, its loose-covered sofa, Persian carpets, painting of a Dutch landscape, cut glass, rosewood table nests, brass standard lamps, Chinese vases, miscellaneous nick-nacks and an array of intricately woven cushion covers depicting English rural scenes purchased from the Needlewoman Shop in Regent Street on shopping expeditions during visits to London. The only Indian touch would appear to be the fresh marigold garlands on the portraits of deceased family, otherwise the room could be anywhere: the décor, style, and even lifestyle inherited from the previous rulers of India, and maintained by the new ones – the new brown sahibs!

Outside a car rumbles into the drive, crackling the gravel under its wheels. Through the net curtains I can see that it is an official car – and can infer the rest: that Aunt Pushpa's daughter, Radha, and son-in-law, Vikram, are in town. Quite likely my cousin-brother has timed some official business in Delhi to fit in neatly with the family business of weddings! In India everyone knows the primacy of family matters! The driver is emptying the boot of the morning's shopping and though he has opened all the doors of the car, no one has alighted from it. 'Of course there is no big mystery about that, is there, Nanaji?' I ask my grandfather's portrait on the table. 'They're probably just immersed in conversation, and after all, why strain yourself when you've got servants to strain themselves for you!'

'Aha, Meera! You're here! We were sitting in the car waiting for you to arrive. We didn't see Sita's car. Where's Sita? And how are you! Come, let me at least embrace you.' My cousin, Radha, throws her parcels down on to a stool as she crosses the room, followed by her two grown-up daughters.

'I'm Neena. Hello, Aunty!' says my first niece.

'Hello, Aunty, I'm Gita,' says the second.

'And I'm Meera!' I reply, to which both of them say, 'Oooh, Aunty,' and release a coo-like giggle sounding a bit like an earlier model of Sita's noncommittal laugh.

'Accha, Meera, rani! You're here!' Aunt Pushpa comes striding in followed by Aunt Daya. 'Sita not with you? Eh? Where's Sita?'

'She couldn't come, Aunty. She had something fixed up.'

'Huh! Something fixed up, eh? Imagine her inviting you and having something fixed up! And especially when you're here for such a short time only.'

As I wonder if I should say something in Sita's defence, the talk in the room has already moved on. Radha tells me that we are all going to have lunch at the club and Aunt Daya tries to find out what arrangements are to be made for the driver's lunch.

'Ask Baby!' shrugs Aunt Pushpa, indicating her fifty-year-old daughter with a nod of her chin.

'Give him lunch here, Aunty. It's such a long drive back to the canteen.'

'Aha! But we don't pay for petrol, and we do pay for lunch!' throws in Pushpa.

'Hun,' retorts Aunt Daya indignantly under her breath. 'Someone pays! Government pays! People pay! Country pays. Hun! I'll tell Lakshmi to call him.'

'Tell him to hurry, Aunty, we've got to get to the club. And you girls, hurry up and put away your packets and get ready.' Radha sorts out the shopping as she speaks. 'It's a government car,' she tells me conspiratorially. 'We've got it for the whole day! Free!' she adds, in case I do not fully understand.

'Accha, what's this? Whose is this?' Aunt Pushpa finds my bag of boxes from the morning's shopping at the Hanuman Mandir.

'Oh, those are my boxes.'

'Boxes of what?'

'Just bangles and nick-nacks. Sita got them for Maya, but she got a bit carried away and got – '

It is the expression on Aunt Pushpa's face that interrupts me. It would seem I have touched a nerve. She purses her lips.

'I've been wanting to get something for Maya too,' she starts, 'but all the time there is somebody, or some work for someone . . . '

'But, Aunty, really it's not necess– '

'Three times to Old Delhi for Mrs Kapur,' Aunt Pushpa raises her voice to make her point that she does not wish to be interrupted. 'Then my car had to go to the garage . . . and I had to beg lifts to get around, and now there's the wedding and Baby and the children have come. Everybody wants me to do their work, give them advice. And today the girls wanted to do their shopping. I never get any time . . . '

'We could all go to the Christmas Bazaar after lunch!' says Gita as Aunt Pushpa pauses for breath.

'What's that?' I ask as my contribution to the gear change.

'Ooh, you don't know the Christmas Bazaar?'

'Then we must go this afternoon . . . '

'It's very crowded . . . '

'You can rest, Radha . . . Stay on at the club.'

'I've been wanting to get a shawl from the Tibetans . . . '

'We'll all go this afternoon . . . '

130

'I say, are you girls ready? The driver will be finished and ready before you are! Imagine! Grown-up girls and I still have to be after them . . . '

'What do you think Maya would like?' Aunt Pushpa asks as we walk to the car. My mind is flooded with possibilities as I try to imagine what.

'Would she like something to eat? Something to wear? Or an object to put in her room?'

'Well, I think she'd like an object . . . ' I try to remember Maya's room.

'What sort of an object?'

Bibiji sitting at her puja comes to mind. 'A murthi maybe. Yes, that's right. A Saraswati! She's wanted that, a figure of the goddess Saraswati with the book and Veena in her hands . . . '

'Achaa, she likes the goddess Saraswati!' Aunt Daya's voice lilts up with pleasure, and her eyes sparkle.

'A Saraswati?' The two girls sound astonished – almost dismissive!

'What on earth would she want to do with a Saraswati,' exclaims Aunt Pushpa.

'Well, Maya is a schoolgirl with musical aspirations – and Saraswati is the goddess of learning.'

'Why don't you get her a Lakshmi! She's the goddess of wealth. I'm sure she'd like that better,' suggests Radha.

'And I know where you can get very nice Lakshmis; they've also got Durga riding on her tiger . . . but I can't remember having seen any Saraswatis.'

'Saraswati is more popular in Bengal or in the south, Meera, not in Delhi. Here it's mostly Lakshmi.'

Power or wealth, I observe, but not learning!

'In any case, we'll see what we can find. But it will have to be another day – we won't find any Saraswatis at the Christmas Bazaar!'

'No, no. That we won't. We certainly won't find any Saraswatis at the Christmas Bazaar!' Everyone laughs –

131

except for Aunt Daya, who looks absently, and a bit sadly, out of the window.

'There are lovely gardens at the club, Meera Aunty.'

'Yes, there's a rose garden and a Mogul garden . . . '

' . . . and a front lawn and a back lawn . . . '

'Mama, can we have lunch on the lawn?'

'Yes, but after we've found Papa. We must find Papa first.'

. . . maybe he's tucked away in the English garden – for there must be an English garden! An English country garden! How did the song go? The words are lost but the melody remains. I hum it under my breath as we enter the club: stately, spacious, polished, privileged . . .

Inherited from the British these clubs were set up by them to keep themselves to themselves, together, and to maintain their mystique! Indians were not allowed! Ruling involved cutting yourself off, making yourselves a cut above, a super élite, not least of all this was to project position and privilege on to others . . . ah yes, the style remains, the system maintained . . .

Aunt Pushpa detaches herself from us as we enter, to join a group of ladies in the centre of the hall. My cousin-brother Vikram approaches us.

'Aha, aha.' He offers me a formal embrace. 'Good to see you, my dear. Good to see you. Will you have something? What will you have?'

Chips and tomato sauce, please, is what I used to say! And now I live in the land of chips and tomato sauce and never touch the stuff. The land of clubs too, but then there I do not belong to the world of clubs . . . and here?

'We'll have lunch on the lawn. Girls go and tell your nani where we'll be. Come Aunty, come Meera. You'll join us, ji?'

'Han han. You go, I'll come,' replies Vikram.

Radha glides along graciously, assuming all the appropriate mannerisms of belonging to the club.

Outside the sun is hot and bright. We find a table and Radha sinks into the chair, turning her head and nodding at acquaintances. The bearer comes and takes our orders.

'Nothing like Delhi in the winter!' exclaims Radha. Aunt Daya nods her head in agreement and anticipation – having been persuaded through Neena's insistence to order a whole plate of chips and tomato sauce, all for herself! What indulgence! She tries to contain the quiver of delight in the turn of her mouth – probably she is reminding herself that these are transient pleasures, belonging to the world of 'maya', or illusion, from which she is quite detached – or trying to be – being a sanyasin at heart. The others join us as lunch is served. The bearer presents a chit to my brother-in-law. He signs it. Money is never exchanged at the club! Oh dear no! Filthy lucre! Here one simply signs. Only a member can sign – so only a member can order. One is either a member or a non-member. You either belong or you don't belong. Though you can be a guest, like me and Aunt Daya. Of course, not anyone can become a member of the club. 'Who can?' I ask, to find I have pressed the button of a familiar conversation piece, as everyone fills me in – except Aunt Daya who just nods her head, raising her eyebrows and widening her eyes at appropriate moments and at the same time slowly savouring her chips as though they were just reward for her attention.

'Of course, it used to be a lot more exclusive.'

'Ooh,' murmurs Aunt Daya.

'Oh yes, definitely. A lot more exclusive!'

'I mean in the old days you went home and changed before coming out to the club.'

'You see, in the British days when they first changed their rules to allow in some Indian members, you could only get in if you belonged to the top echelons of the services, or were a prince or nawab. Very exclusive.'

'Yes, that's right. It used to be only the members of the topmost élite.'

'Nani, Grandfather and you were members during the British period, weren't you?'

'Oh, yes! Oh, yes! We certainly were. We were among the

first handfuls. Strict protocol used to be maintained in those days. British style.'

'Of course it's still very difficult to become a member, and an application can take years and years.'

'Accchhhaaa, reeeally!' Aunt Daya is stretching her chips to last a long time.

' . . . yes, in the beginning it used to be the top echelons of the services – army, navy, airforce, civil – you know what I mean. Some businessmen, but only the very top. There were also people from the professions – barristers, doctors, accountants, journalists . . . '

'Vikram used to be on the membership panel,' Radha tells us proudly.

'Of course there still are priority groups and their applications can get processed quicker. There was this doctor from the All-India Medical Institute and his application took only three years – that's the same time it takes to get a telephone . . . '

'But still there are lots of novohs now, aren't there, Mama?'

'Hmmmm?' nods Aunt Daya as she ruminates. 'What's novohs?'

'You young people coming out with new words all the time . . . '

'Novoh rishes! You know, Nani. The people who have just got rich.'

'As we've got poorer!' laughs Vikram.

'I say, Meera? You've hardly eaten anything. Are you all right?'

'She must have had some chaat at the Hanuman Mandir,' replies Aunt Pushpa, tucking in. 'Eat chaat and you fall ill.'

'We're going to the Christmas Bazaar after lunch, Papa.'

'Good, good. Take the car. You going too, Radha?'

'No, no. I'm going to rest. They'll drop me off on their way.'

Twenty-four

'Come! We're there!' Aunt Pushpa is already out of the car. I look out at what seems like chaos and crowd before I realise that I am once again in Janpath, the People's Way of today which used to be the old Queensway of yesterday! Well, of people it certainly is full, combining into a teeming colourful confusion. For Janpath, crowded at the best of times, now looks bursting – everything in movement: the people on the pavement, garments in the wind, glitter in the sun! What words? Variety, vitality, abundance, anarchy . . .

'Systems!' Usha had said not far from here as she sliced her Chicken à la Kiev spilling forth its golden butter. Systems! But then isn't India . . . isn't India – what? . . . and what isn't India! Maybe even the so-called confusion is nothing more than simply the lack of ability to discern, to differentiate . . . from all the different systems and possibilities and ways of being – surely there must be one for me! Oh yes! There'll be one I can fit into . . .

'Come!' cries out Aunt Pushpa as she steps off the pavement and into the street, firmly ignoring the traffic lights and crossing a bit further up. She pulls her granddaughters behind her and waves her arms to stop the traffic and impress upon everyone her right to be where she is by virtue of her being a car owner, hence road owner, as well as being a member of the privileged class that inherited India! India roars on around her, deafened and deafening. I keep turning to watch her, spritelier in her seventies than either of her granddaughters in their twenties! Aunt Daya meanwhile is pulling me to the crossing, mumbling under her breath that the traffic lights have been installed for good reason, and that her sister should set a better example to her granddaughters!

'How are we going to advance properly if the new generation is not taught to care! Everyone in India is advancing in their own directions.'

On the pavement the crowd looks dense and impenetrable and advancing nowhere at all. Yet, as we approach it, it stretches like elastic to receive us and we are soon absorbed to jostle our way along with the visitors, the locals, the pedlars, the beggars, the truth seekers – for Janpath caters for the many Indias and the many visions of India. India, which incorporates, includes, absorbs, and where everything – all forms, all centuries, all differences exist, co-exist, collide and the ancient bullock cart transports the modern computer . . . FIXED PRICE catches my eye. I recognise my export-quality shoe shop but there is no time to stop. I feel the flapping of the heels against the soles of my feet.

'Look! This is India!' exclaims Aunt Pushpa as we reach her, savouring the hustle and the colour and the crowds around her.

'Shall we agree to meet at the car in case one of us gets lost,' I suggest.

'We won't lose you . . . ' starts Aunt Daya.

'Good idea, Meera! I want to go and see the shawls. Want to come?'

'Shall I take Meera Aunty to see the bargains?' suggests Gita.

I follow Gita to see the Christmas Bazaar bargains, though it is hardly possible to see anything through the crowd. Gita, however, seems to be able to navigate through them with a definite sense of direction. I follow.

'Panjarupeypanjarupeypanjarupeypancharupeypan,' trails the monotone cry from the direction we are approaching. A street seller is revealed standing there holding up garments, gesticulating and hardly stopping for breath. It registers that he's calling out their price – panj rupey! Five rupees! Surely

136

not! It couldn't be! Five rupees – twenty-five pence! Impossible!

'How much is this?' I pick up a blouse, quite a nice one at that. In reply the vendor stretches out a hand to clearly indicate five. Then pointing to an adjacent pile, he stretches out both hands to signify ten all the while carrying on shouting in his monotone: 'Panjrupey panjrupey . . . '

'So cheap? How? I mean the cloth would cost more than that! And without the cost of the stitching!'

'They're export rejects, Aunty!' Gita tells me, as though stating the obvious.

'What's that?'

'An export order which either fell through . . . or there were too many pieces . . . or something wasn't quite right. I don't know but . . . something like that. Then they come here and are sold cheap.'

'You're telling me!'

Export quality rejects! Export – Quality! Import – Mediocrity! India is free! Free – to export the best, home quality the rest! Tangled clothes, tangled crowd. And what about the monkeys? Were they grabbed and trapped and sorted into export quality as well!

'Meera, Masi? Aunty shall we go back and find Nani?' There is concern in Gita's voice.

Gita leads. I follow, getting dizzier with the noise – in my head impressions and confusions, and around, the loud, pressing crowd.

Export quality smoothly fitting. Home quality pinching slipping. Find yourself a place in the boom business of India's fastest-growing industry . . . for in India there are those who eat or those who get consumed! And how many I wonder are consumed to feed one . . . for if over half the population live below the poverty line . . . and over half of those remaining live just above it – then those who eat must consume a lot! What happened to the idealism, the promise of that 'tryst with destiny' that we were brought up to be inspired by. That

137

'noble Mansion of free India' that was supposed to have been built . . . for all its citizens? Is this it? And what the hell and who the hell am I . . . so far away. 'Talking like a visitor' as Savitri would say.

'Aw c'mon, Maw!' Comes a girl's voice from my side. 'You can get all this in the US!'

I stop in my thoughts and turn to look at the speaker. A young Indian American girl, jeaned and sneakered. Disidentifying. Her mother carries on looking at some cloth and tells her in Punjabi that she is just coming – to which the girl replies, 'Aw, Maw!'

Parvati! How scratched your face must be! Another story comes to mind – an image from it – how does the story go?

'I say, Meera! Baby! What's happened to you? Are you not well? You look pale . . . ' Aunt Daya asks anxiously as she locates us in the crowd.

'I don't know, Aunty. I'm just . . . I don't know what . . . I don't know what I am!'

'You look tired. We'll go home now. Take her to the car, Gita, rani. I'll go and find Sister.'

Twenty-five

The sun shines hot, a glow of heat on my back. Shadows around. The wedding party moves along. We are the baraat – the groom's family – on our way to the bride's house. We are the honoured guests, to be feasted and fed and fussed over. We are many. The whole family has turned up, glittering in expensive silks, shawls, brocades and jewels. 'All show . . . all show . . . ' Where's Bibiji? I turn to see – but my look confronts the brilliance of the sun, the crowd is dissolved into anonymity.

The groom rides on a horse. Bridegrooms always ride horses – like the ancient kings and heroes of old. And the gods. Yes, the gods, too, ride all sorts: horses and bulls and ganders and tigers and lions.

'If your parents' membership to the club had not elapsed before they died then you can get automatic membership,' someone tells me, a cousin I haven't met until now.

'We can stop at the club on our way to the wedding and find out.' It's Radha's voice. I turn, and Ravibhai smiles at me.

'Hello, Ravibhai!'

'Hello, rat-catcher!'

The horse that the groom rides . . . haven't I seen it before? . . . At that shop . . . the Cottage?

'Funny, I thought it was a wooden horse!'

'Ha! Ha! Trust you!' Savitri laughs.

'But it *is* the same horse you saw . . . the wooden one,' says Sita.

'But then how does it move?'

'Ha, ha, ha! This is India.'

'Anything and everything can happen in India.'

'And if it doesn't, you can make it,' says Sanjay.

' . . . especially when you know your way around,' adds Ravibhai. We all laugh.

Ha ha ha ha ha! We are the wedding party. The baraat. On our way to be feasted and fussed over. We will be given sweets and gifts as well as the daughter of the house. She will be all coy and cry. She has to cry. If she doesn't she'll never live it down, and learn her way around in her new family. All the women will cry. First on her side and then maybe even on this side – as they remember their own seven steps around the fire. The fire that burns – burns away and purifies. And Agni the fire god witnesses, propitiated by the offerings of ghee, camphor . . . all thrown into the fire – a sudden darkening, a burst of flame, a cloud of smoke and the fire burns brighter – burning away fears, purifying desires.

We are walking along the river bank. On sand. A sandy river bank. The wedding party, alive with chatter – gossip, news, views, deals, transactions – bouncing down the line, or floating up into the sky. Words and voices merging and disappearing.

The horse steps into the river, no, on to the river. On to the river? Yes we are walking on the river. The river is frozen. A solid surface beneath our feet. But how? A frozen river? In the hot sun? It is hot. I am hot.

'Anything and everything can happen in India . . . '

'And when you know your way around, you know how to do things and find things . . . '

Everyone laughs. Comfortable and secure in the knowledge that they know – how to do and where to find. The family laughs. I join them laughing and walking along the smooth surface of the frozen river. But further down, it would appear the river is not frozen. No, further down the river flows – people slip and falter, dip in and swim. We all laugh. We are the family who know our way around. I laugh

140

and look around and down, where the river moves. But isn't that . . . Kesru? And my parents? My husband and daughter? And . . . surely that's Dr Shankar? Why are they there and why am I here? Why and what am I laughing about . . .

'Meera! Meera! Where are you going? Come back! Come back otherwise your membership to the club will elapse . . . elapse . . . elapse . . . '

'Dr Shankar . . . Dr Shankar . . . '

'Hello, Dr Shankar. Can you hear me now? These Delhi telephones are so bad. Meera is here. Yes, from London. She's fallen ill. She's running a fever. Yes. Acchaa. Thank you very much. Then we'll see you soon. Goodbye, ji.'

'He's coming?'

'He's coming.'

'Now?'

'Now.'

'Good. At least that's one thing settled. She'll be happy to see him too. Such good friends they were, her father and Dr Shankar.'

'I should never have left her. So pale . . . Poor Vidya's little girl . . . '

'Ooof oh! Stop crying Daya. She's our Meera and she was perfectly well yesterday morning . . . Maybe she ate something . . . '

'Han, that's it. Must have had some chaat. That's it. Pushpa bhenji even said so. At the club also she didn't hardly have any lunch at all. She had chaat and now she's ill! These children never listen! She looked so ill when I found her at the Christmas Bazaar. Han, definitely she had chaat.'

'She's sleeping?'

'Han han. She's sleeping. Running a fever . . . '

What's running? . . . the fever? . . . Meera? Meera! . . . Who is Meera! Who am I? I am running . . . where to? where from? who could tell me? do I know? Follow the fever. Follow me!

Twenty-six

Flickering light. Fire. Fire burns, purifies and flickers light. Where am I? Ah yes! Meera has fallen ill! The oil lamp on the dressing table flickers. From outside, too, the light also flickers through the curtains of the darkened room, revealing their colour – deep turquoise blue, like the blue on the peacock's feathers. Flickers of blue in the sunlight, but when I close my eyes the blue changes to orange. If the curtains were orange would I then see blue when I closed my eyes? Was my dream in colour? Oh Mama and Papa! How I wish you were still here . . .

I am alone in the room. How late is it? What's the time? What's Time? Tick-tock. My watch. On my wrist. Too heavy to move. Aunt Daya comes into the room. Tiptoeing. She salutes the oil lamp and rearranges the flowers. A temporary shrine has been created on the dressing table – two figures, a lamp, a few flowers, smoking incense – and the place now is invested with special meaning through the power of faith. How simple and how difficult! Aunt Daya tiptoes over to the bed.

'Rani? You've woken up?'

'Hmmm.'

She touches my forehead. 'You're still running fever. I'll be back. I'll get you a drink.' She tiptoes out of the room.

One of the large armchairs from the drawing room has been placed in my room. Aunt Daya cools my drink by pouring it from the cup into the saucer and then carefully back from the saucer into the cup. All the while she talks, telling me that Bibiji had sat in my room 'right up until lunchtime', that Dr Shankar had come by and would be coming again, and that Pushpa had called to say that Ravibhai was back and could get my reservation to London postponed because he knew how to get things done . . .

'Is it after lunch now?'

'Oh, yes! Lunch was long time ago. But yours is there . . . '

'I don't want to eat.'

'But you must have something to eat.'

'Later, maybe. But not now.'

'Dr Shankar will be back soon. He runs a free clinic, did you know? Oh yes, he does seva, and looks after the poor. Here drink this . . . '

'But . . . '

'Drink, drink.'

'I had such a strange dream . . . '

'You had a fever,' replies Aunt Daya, as though that explains everything.

Dr Shankar stands by my bed and smiles, reminding me of my father and making me feel like a child. A tall, thin man with grey hair and ageless eyes – penetrating and gentle – he looks at me intently as he feels my pulse and questions me about my symptoms, nodding his head all the while. Aunt Daya also nods and her lips move quickly and silently – probably murmuring some old prayer or other, I decide with a twitch of irritation.

'So, meri Meeru! Tell me, why have you fallen ill?'

Meri Meeru is what my father used to call me. A sob surges from my stomach surfacing into a small sigh and a film over my eyes.

'How can I know . . . ?'

'She had chaat.' Aunt Daya tells him.

'Your stomach is upset?'

'No. And I didn't have any chaat. I don't know what happened. It's just so confusing.'

'What's confusing?'

'I don't know! India? Me? I've been rushing around, meeting the family, going here and there, searching, trying to find things out and now I'm even more lost than when I came. Oh, Uncle! Sometimes . . . I don't even know . . . who I am!'

Aunt Daya wipes her eyes with the edge of her sari. Dr Shankar laughs.

'Aha, my Meeru! That's a big enough question to confuse anyone! Who am I?'

He sits down on the edge of my bed and strokes back my hair. His hands feel cool and smooth. 'You know of Ramana Maharishi? The great saint? Well, he only ever asked himself just that one question in his search for the ultimate understanding of human existence: who am I? Nothing else!'

'Well, I'm no saint and neither am I looking for ultimates or whatevers. I'm just an ordinary person. And I'm fed up of all this saint-paint philosophising. In India there's always a saint or a story to diffuse and confuse everything further. It makes me tired to think about it.'

'Well, there's no need to think about it all now. And some questions . . . are best just left. Here, open your mouth.' He pours a dose of sweet powder under my tongue. 'Now just allow this to melt away in your mouth as you melt away into sleep.'

'Uncle?' I say, half melting away.

'Yes.'

'I had such a . . . strange dream.'

He nods thoughtfully. 'Yes, yes. Sleep for now and then tell me all about it when you wake.' The smooth hands close my eyes.

'Dr Sahib, Dr Sahib. What should she eat?'

'Has she said she's hungry?'

'No, no. That's just it. She doesn't want anything!'

'Then give her nothing!'

'Nothing, Dr Sahib?'

'Nothing. Nothing unless she wants something.'

'And Dr Sahib. Pushpa bhenji says she can get a

144

postponement of the journey with a certificate. You see Meera's booked to leave in six days!'

'The fever will be gone by tomorrow or at the most the day after. When it is gone, she will know what she wants to do. The certificate can be made then . . . '

I melt away deep down, into a place where I know what to do . . . and where I can find a way to stay . . . where I know I want to be . . . where I can sleep . . .

Twenty-seven

It is morning. I half open my eyes and listen for the familiar sound cues. But the house is strangely silent. My watch will tell me what I need to know. I start to pull my arm out from under the bedclothes . . .

'Namaste, Meera biji.'

Minoo is squatting on the floor beside my bed.

'What are you doing here?'

'Nothing.'

'You're always doing nothing!'

'They said I should watch over you and tell them when you woke up and get you anything you wanted.'

'Anything I wanted?'

'Yes, anything you wanted.'

'Where is everybody?'

'Bibiji is having her breakfast and Daya biji went to Mrs Verma's house but she'll be back just now!' She gets up.

'And where are you off to?'

'To tell them you've woken up of course! I'll be back.' She cradles a bundle in her arms.

'What's that you're holding?'

She beams. 'I'll be back!' She charges out. Bright button eyes sparkling delight.

The tap-tap-tapping of the stick tells me that Bibiji is on her way.

'Hel-lo, rani! Hel-lo hel-lo!' Bibiji almost sings as she enters. 'How are you feeling? Are you better? Minoo, go and get my books and bags and a small table.' She eases herself

146

into the armchair and tries unsuccessfully to find a place for her walking stick. 'And put this stick away,' she adds.

Minoo, who has carefully placed her bundle on the spare bed, takes the stick and places it alongside before tearing off to fulfil the other errands.

'Go quietly! Go quietly!' urges Bibiji in vain as Minoo clatters noisily away. 'Noisy child!' Bibiji shakes her head as though shaking out the noise. 'So. How about you? You're better?'

'I'm a bit chilly.'

'Chilly, eh? We'll get a fire. Minoo, Minoo! Get the fire from my puja room. She can't hear. I'll tell her when she comes. Dr Shankar told us there was nothing to worry about and the fever would go. He'll be here soon. And you slept all right?'

'Hmm, I slept well. The night before, though, I had a strange . . . drea– '

But Bibiji is busy settling down and issuing new instructions to Minoo to bring the fire, a shawl, find Aunt Daya. 'Have you had breakfast? Will you have something more?'

'Some tea.'

'And tell Chandu to bring some tea for Meera bibiji and this time remember to go off quietly.' Minoo grins sheepishly.

Bibiji's chair has, as usual, been placed so as to give her maximum view of the room. As I sip my tea and watch her writing industriously in her book I wonder quite how and when this new arrangement was made, if she had it moved to its strategic position or if the servants had just known exactly what to do. Minoo, now freed of her errands, has retrieved her bundle and settled down with it near the fire. She catches me looking at her and holds up her pink baby doll, now with blackened hair. 'Parvati!' she tells me all twinkle and smiles. 'Isn't she beautiful! Shall I bring her to you?'

'Later Minoo, later. Let Meera bibiji drink her tea quietly. She needs quiet and rest to get well.' Bibiji does not stop writing as she speaks.

147

'There's a Parvati devi there,' Minoo tells me pointing to one of the figures on the dressing-table altar.

'Ram ram, rani, ram ram. And there's a Krishanji too.' Aunt Daya comes in slightly breathless. 'The Parvati used to be your mother's.'

'Oooof!' I sigh. Involuntarily and loudly. Putting down my tea I slide into the bedclothes, as though to protect myself from the onslaught of yet more memories, feelings, stories.

'Rani?'

'Meera?'

'Are you all right?'

'Is anything wrong?'

My aunts both look startled and worried.

'Have you pain?' suggests Aunt Daya.

Have I got pain? 'Pain? No, not pain . . . something else . . . '

'Tell us, rani.'

'Han, han. Tell us,' repeats Aunt Daya as she sits down on the spare bed and is obstructed by Bibiji's stick. She moves it out of the way, putting it across the pillow.

'There's nothing to tell really. I just remembered something.'

'It's because I said it was your mother's murthi,' nods Aunt Daya, her eyes brimming over.

'No, no, Aunty. Well not exactly.'

'Tell us anyway.' Bibiji's voice is deep and strong. Aunt Daya raises her eyebrows and opens her eyes wider in anticipation. She moves further back on to the bed. Bibiji's stick rolls down beside her, she looks at it, and leaves it there and returns her attention to me.

'All the while that I've been here, I've often been bombarded by old memories, meanings, stories – as though they are floating around . . . in the dust . . . ' Yes, the dust – always there, like a halo, a mirror image, a shadow, all pervasive, ready to overwhelm. 'And when we were at the Christmas Bazaar, and there were all those people running, pushing, grabbing, all those things, all that . . . I remem-

bered this story of Parvati with her face all scratched that
Mama told me . . . it all collided and now it just came back to
me with the feeling of then . . . ' The feeling of then? The
feeling of when? When Mama first told me the story? The
Christmas Bazaar? Or just now . . . ?

'Aah-ha! I know which story! I remember! I know the
story. Shall I tell it?' Aunt Daya is still wide eyed.

'Tell, tell, tell,' coos Minoo.

'Are you listening, Meera, do you want to hear it, rani?'

No, I think. But how could I say it. Aunt Daya is already
preparing herself. She takes Bibiji's stick from beside her
and slips it under the bed, and sits down more comfortably.

'Tell . . . ' says Minoo.

'I'm telling, I'm telling . . . Once . . . ' She starts. I close
my eyes to cut myself off.

'Yes. Once Parvati and little Ganesh were at home and
little Ganesh was playing around, as children do, playing at
this and playing at that, and then he saw a cat and wanted to
play with it.'

Bibiji writes, Minoo nods.

'So he called the cat. But the cat ran away. So he chased
the cat here there and everywhere. Up the tree, through the
garden, under the furniture, around the house . . . He would
catch it and grab it and pull it and squeeze it and scratch it –
but the cat always managed to slip away. Soon, Ganesh,
because he was only a child, even though a god, got fed up of
this game and stopped. He was also feeling a bit tired by
now, so he went over to sit in his mother's lap – because
Parvati was sitting there. So when he was sitting in Parvati's
lap, he looked at her – and he was shocked! Because what
did he see?'

Bibiji writes. Minoo shakes her head questioningly.

'Well, what he saw was that the goddess Parvati, his
beloved mother, was all dishevelled and scratched and
bruised and hurt. And little Ganeshji was so shocked, he
jumped down from her lap and said, very angry and very
upset, "Whoooo, but whoo did this to you?" He was all

149

ready to go and defend – even avenge his mother! "Whoo did this to you," he asked. And the goddess Parvati looked at him sweetly and replied, "You did."

' "Me? What do you mean me?" said little Ganeshji, "How could I? And when?"

'And Parvati smiled and replied, "You did it to me just now, when you were playing with the cat!" '

Minoo nods and Bibiji writes and nods and Aunt Daya joins them and all the heads go bob, bob, bob. I quickly close my half-open eyes.

'And then Ganeshji understood.'

'I understand too,' chirps Minoo.

'Very good. Very good,' drones the baritone.

Stories! Always stories! India is full of stories! Stories to amuse, to confuse, to justify, to diffuse . . . probably all the objects in this room have a story and every particle of dust belonged to some other story . . .

'Stories are cheap and plentiful but of what use are they and who do they feed?'

'Hai, rani!' Aunt Daya looks hurt at my abrupt intervention.

'All I can say is that Parvati must be pretty bruised and beaten and confused and hungry if the state of the country is anything to go by. What meaning do all these stories have when the people are still so poor?'

'Just because the people are poor does not mean that stories have no meaning, Meera,' Bibiji says gently, writing all the while.

Aunt Daya comes over to my bed and touches my forehead. 'It's the fever,' she explains. 'She's still running fever. Rest, rani. There's been too much noise for you.'

Indeed, indeed. Too much noise. Minoo cradles her doll protectively and avoids my look.

'It is just the politicians who are ruining the country and understanding nothing except their own drunkenness and greed for power and money,' Aunt Daya recites like a formula. 'But you rest now, Meera. Rest until lunchtime. Dr

Shankar will be here soon.' She gets up to go, first stopping at the dressing-table shrine, lightly touching each of the statues and then bringing her hand to her forehead. As she leaves the room her step falters slightly – just like my mother's used to do . . .

I close my eyes as a cold and hollow shiver runs through me. I feel limp, just like that first time – when I got the news that my father, too, had died, just three months after my mother, just fourteen days before I was to see him again. Suddenly everything was lost . . . everything! And now . . . I've even lost India . . .

'Where have you gone and lost it now? whispers Bibiji.

'But I put it here. I know I did,' replies Minoo.

'Shh, not so loudly. You never look where you put things.'

'But I did, Biji, I put it there,' whispers Minoo.

'Then where is it?'

'If you're looking for the stick, it's under the bed.' I cover myself with the bedclothes and turn away.

Shuffle, scrape, tap-tap-tap. The door closes and the room is silent.

Twenty-eight

I wake up once again to find Dr Shankar sitting in Bibiji's chair reading a newspaper.

'Uncle?'

'Aha!' He looks up, his eyes clear and sharp. 'You're awake.'

'Yes. I keep waking and sleeping and not knowing if it's yesterday or today, a dream or reality.'

Dr Shankar laughs, folds away the paper and comes over to sit on the spare bed. 'Vah, vah, Meera! Such observations you make! Such . . . what was it? Paint-faint philosophy! Are you better?'

I sigh in reply.

'Fever's down but I'll give you one more dose and soon it will be gone.'

And will my confusion be gone too, I wonder, but do not ask, as I watch Dr Shankar carefully choose from among the bottles and boxes in his well-worn but meticulously arranged case . . . 'Why have you fallen ill,' he'd asked. Does one fall ill for a reason?

'Open your mouth . . . let it melt under your tongue and don't eat or drink anything for half an hour.'

And soon you'll be as right as rain! That's what I used to tell Maya.

'Are you off now?' I ask. There must be a twinge in my tone for his reply is quite tender.

'No, no, Meeru. I'll stay with you until after lunch, then I must go to the clinic – I have some people to see – but I will come back in the evening.' He looks at me firmly yet with gentle concern.

'You asked me yesterday why I fell ill. Does one fall ill for a reason?'

'Yes, one can do, one can do. Sometimes in life, things that go wrong are trying to put something right.'

'Feels like a riddle! I don't like riddles and stories any more. It all feels like noise.'

Dr Shankar doesn't reply; instead he nods his head.

'I don't understand India any more, either!'

He raises his eyebrows into a question mark. 'Is it necessary for you to understand it?'

'I feel that it's closed its doors on me. When I was a child and even later . . . when I would come to India, it was like magic . . . so full of promise and possibilities and idealism. It was like a wonderful cake full of layers, colours, aromas, flavours, soft and light and rich with infinite possibilities . . .'

Dr Shankar listens.

'And now – it's as though the cream has become so thick and top heavy that it has crushed everything else into a crust, and made the cake sickening.'

'Sickening, Meera?'

'Well, I feel sick. Parties, hotels, clubs, sham and show, me, me, mine, and nobody cares. It's as though the idealism and promise has just . . . dissolved . . . into the dust. It's all so disturbing. You know, I think that's why I fell ill. Could that be?'

'It could.' He nods his head. 'Disturbance in the mind can make us physically ill, but rest your mind for now. Stop thinking about all this – then when you get better the whole of you will get better. Don't worry, Meeru. The promise and idealism you remember – it's all still there and can be found – there are many Indias, you know!'

'So I keep being told!' I reply wearily.

'But it is true. It's true. There's sham and show as you say, but much else as well. And India exists in you too – trust that, and other things will become more clear.'

153

'Like what?'

He laughs. 'Like . . . whatever needs to . . . the other Indias?'

'I don't really understand . . . You make it seem so simple.'

'Don't try so hard to understand, Meeru.' Dr Shankar laughs lightly. 'Just let it be. Understanding will follow. It's not India that closes its doors. Only we do that.'

'I needed so much to find . . . to connect – instead I've only found out how much I've lost and how little freedom and choice is left.'

'Choice is always there. And freedom too, and responsibil- ity . . . '

'Sometimes you sound just like Papa. Oh, Uncle, I've remembered them so much; so much . . . is gone – so much is lost!'

'Not lost. Things go, things change, and they also remain . . . something does . . . the vibration remains.' Dr Shankar nods with certainty.

'Like the stories. The stories that just seem to come . . . from dust. But still they're not here to talk to and it's so . . . hard.'

'But of course it's hard . . . but no one can think or choose for you.' Dr Shankar's look is incisive. 'Only you can do that. Only you can become what you know yourself to be.' To my puzzled look he adds, 'For that you need to create some silence.' He breathes deeply.

Always riddles and more riddles it feels. What I know myself to be! But it's a nice formulation . . . What I . . . know myself . . . to be? A silence hangs in the room. A silence enclosed within the sounds of the midday routine all around . . .

'You know Uncle, I had a strange dream. In my dream . . . I think I made a . . . sort of choice.'

'What was your dream?'

'I dreamed I was walking on this frozen river in the warm sun with the baraat. The whole family was there. Even

154

though I didn't see them all I knew they were there, at least most of them were. I felt included but I didn't feel I belonged. Then I saw that further down the river was not frozen and that people were even slipping. They were ordinary people, like Kesru and Chandu, and among them were my parents, Maya, Martin, and you were there too – and then . . . I walked over towards all of you and away from the frozen river, towards the river that flowed. What do you think was the meaning of all that?'

Dr Shankar shakes his head. 'I don't know. But how did you feel?'

'It felt the right thing to do. And I felt right doing it.'

'Then that's good. After all, the natural movement of water is to flow . . . '

'That's right. So it is! I followed a natural movement! Yes, I'd like to think that I did make that choice . . . But then again – what did I choose?'

Dr Shankar laughs. Such a refreshing laugh. 'Maybe you walked towards the other Indias.'

'But I walked away – I left the family . . . '

'You don't have to leave anything – just to include. Like India does, it includes everything.'

Dr Shankar smiles, and his eyes smile and I smile in return.

'It certainly does that! And manages to create the most incredible confusion!' I laugh.

'Ah, Meera! It's nice to hear your laugh and see your smile. The same smile, meri Meeru, my Meeru!'

'I can't help wondering, though, if India won't just remain for me what Krishna was for the other Meera – Meerabai – an interminable search for the unattainable ideal for which she waited and longed and sang endless songs . . . '

'Oh, my Meera! What are you saying! No, no!' Dr Shankar throws his arms up in the air and shakes his head vigorously. 'What a narrow dimension you are reducing Meera to! Meerabai was so much much more. She was a woman of great courage, steadfastness, a free spirit who broke through the narrow confines imposed upon her, of being a princess and a woman, to follow her deepest natural impulse and be what she knew herself to be. She didn't just wait and hope and long, Meeru! Never! Nothing of the kind! She chose to direct her life! She acted! With devotion! With determination! Defiance even!' I watch Dr Shankar's fiery look transform into a thoughtful one, as he adds, softly, 'All these stories and tales that you don't like to hear any more – they are all only little keys to unlock greater meanings, sources of inspiration and understanding of how to direct our lives. To me, increasingly, Meerabai and others like her – be they saints or mystics or revolutionaries or simple people – represent the magic of India. They represent the true spirit that moves the people. My work at the clinic and in the villages has confirmed that. Now, more than ever.'

Dr Shankar's face looks ageless, young and very old at the same time. As he nods his head in reply to his own thoughts, it occurs to me that he too has his own story – connected and rooted in the young and very ancient India. A story of which I know just chapter headings – fiery student leader, freedom fighter, doctor, husband, widower, father, man of the people . . . and my father's friend.

'I remember Papa used to tell me about you and him during the freedom movement.'

Dr Shankar nods gently . . . reminiscing. 'Ah yes! We too had our dreams you know, our whole generation had them, or so it seemed. We had fought hard for our freedom and would now cherish it, make it flower and bloom. We believed we could do anything, for who now could stop us – but ourselves!' He shakes his head. 'We have all known disillusionment . . . that is all part of learning and growth . . . '

We are interrupted by Minoo carrying a plate of food for me and announcing to Dr Shankar that the lunch is being served. 'Yes, yes. I'm coming now. Okay then, Meeru. You rest again after lunch, and I'll see you later. You'll be okay now – in no time.'

I eat my lunch and digest the impressions of the morning – wordlessly into feelings. The 'no time' is now – the running fever has run away. Or so it feels anyway! I half wonder what it is I know myself to be as I watch Minoo playing with her doll. Maya's 'Lovely Sunshine'.

'Come and sit by me, Minoo.'

'You're remembering Maya baby?' she asks with a lilting tone as she slides across the floor.

'Clever monkey aren't you?' I pat her cheek. 'How did you guess?'

'Ha!' she replies cheekily and grins.

'Yes. I was thinking of Maya and that I'll be seeing her soon.' I imagine her chirping around telling me of all her Christmas presents. Thank goodness I had the presence of mind to get all that together before I left – I'm bringing so little back! And Martin! I haven't got anything for him. Maybe someone could pick up a pack of those sandalwood visiting cards. And a cotton pyjama kurta. He'd like that! As I allow images of my life in London to float by without dispelling them, I am reminded that I have not confirmed my arrival as I said I would and wonder what I should do. A letter couldn't possibly reach in time. Cable . . . or . . .

'That will be happy for you.'

'What will?'

'When you are all together again,' states Minoo. 'When Chandu's wife went away to the village it was only supposed to be for three weeks but she didn't come back for three months. She said, when you go home after a long time there's so much to see and do, isn't there Meera bibiji?'

'Yes, Minoo. There is.'

'And you'll go back to your machine?'

'My machine?' I ask, puzzled.

'Yes. The sweeper machine.'

I laugh and put down my plate to allow myself to do so more fully, as I imagine myself returning to embrace my vacuum cleaner! My machine!

'Yes, yes, Minoo, I will go back to my machine and many

other things . . . ' I slide into the bed. 'I'll only know what other things when I'm there.' But whatever they may be I shall try to allow and include them . . .

'You've finished?'

'What? Oh my lunch? Yes, I've finished.'

Minoo takes my plate away and then returns, announcing that she will sing a lullaby for Parvati and me!

'Nini, baby, nini. Makhan roti chini . . . ' She sings in her child's voice the same lullaby my mother used to sing to Maya, and maybe my grandmother sang to her.

At tea time, Aunt Daya assures me, 'Dr Shankar is not only just a very good doctor, he is also such a very good man. So much he does for the poor people. That's why his medicines always work. Isn't that so, Masiji?'

Bibiji nods her head and writes away.

Aunt Daya is all dressed up and ready in silken elegance, waiting to be picked up by Aunt Pushpa to be taken off to the family wedding that evening.

'Such a pity, though, that you'll be missing the wedding. Especially when we're the baraat and don't have to do any work.'

Bibiji throws a critical glance at her niece and then resumes her writing with a shake of the head.

'If you'd come I could have explained the whole ceremony to you.'

'There are always weddings. Such a big family, every year there's at least one!' declares Bibiji.

'I had a dream about the wedding and the baraat.'

'Acchaa? Really?' Aunt Daya raises her eyebrows high and widens her eyes.

'But you weren't there Bibiji. I remember looking for you.'

'No, no, I never go to weddings any more. Too much noise and . . .' The sentence is left incomplete.

'Was I there?' asks Aunt Daya.

'Yes, you were there. I didn't see you. But I know you

158

were there all right.'

My aunt smiles. I look over to the little altar still on the dressing table.

Aunt Pushpa whirlwinds in and out carrying off Aunt Daya and leaving behind her disappointment that I am well enough to catch my plane and that she will not be able to show off her resourcefulness in getting things done.

'Only a few more days, eh, rani.' Bibiji's deep soothing voice re-establishes calm.

'Yes, Bibiji.' Only a few more days. 'I'm a bit disappointed about one thing though.'

'Disappointed? What are you disappointed about?'

'I would have liked to have sent a message saying that I was coming and when. You see I said I'd confirm. Of course I can do that – I can call or cable – but that feels a bit abrupt. I'd have preferred to send a letter.' Especially since I've not written since I've been here, I think, but do not say.

'That can be arranged,' replies Bibiji. 'Your letter can be sent.'

'How?'

'Mrs Rai's son flies to London tonight. He'll take your letter.'

'That's amazing! Do you really think he could?'

'Of course he could. Why not?'

'I could just give him some money for a taxi and they'll take it and deliver it without a problem.'

'A taxi?' Bibiji looks suspicious.

'It's all right you know. That's how it's done over there. I'm always having to send off books and documents in taxis.' An image of my life in London flashes by.

'I don't know about all that. You can discuss it with him. I'll send a message round at once. Mrs Rai was here just half an hour ago. Minoo, Minoo,' she calls as Minoo enters through the door to tell her that the Vakil sahib, her lawyer, has arrived to see her.

'Get your letter ready, rani,' she tells me as she gets up to leave.

Her mischievous tooth gleams and her eyes twinkle. 'It's not only Pushpa who can get things done in this family,' she throws out as she tap-tap-taps away.

I pull out a pen and a blank sheet of paper, to find I am suddenly paralysed as to what to write, as every expression swims and then drowns in my head. I close my eyes and listen to my breathing in an attempt to create a silence. Sure enough, a few minutes later, I know what to do. I pull off the bedclothes, dive across the room and into the cupboard, rummage through my shopping packets and find – the card. Back in bed I look at it again – the picture of the lone figure, carrying a small bag and a musical instrument and walking towards the red-orange fiery glow of the sunset. I open it up and read once again: *I don't know where I'm going, but I'm on my way*. I pick up my pen, and write: 'Home. To myself, and to you. Arriving at Heathrow on the 2nd, a.m. See you then. Meera.'

The letter has been sent. Night has come and Dr Shankar yet again prepares to leave after his evening's visit.

'You know, Uncle. I was thinking earlier, that even though I didn't find what I wanted . . . I found . . . what it is I don't want. I feel that's a first step!'

'It is. It is.'

'And, Uncle, there's one thing else.'

'Yes, Meeru.'

'Before I leave. Will you tell me a story? A story I can take with me – which will unfold meanings . . . '

'A story! You want a story, eh?' He laughs. 'Good! Good! But for that, you must ask one of your aunts to tell you one. And when I come tomorrow you can tell me which one you were told! And tomorrow also, you can get up.'

Twenty-nine

The familiar scene of the garden looks changed. The sun which I soak in feels warmer, the colours brighter, the outlines more distinct, the hues more subtle, and the sound and smells . . . everything seems more real, more alive.

Bibiji sits in her chair and writes, the familiar two-tiered table by her side.

'You know, Aunty, they say that fire burns away and purifies. I think that fevers must do that too. I feel lighter – almost as though some unnecessary weight had just burned away.'

My great-aunt listens and smiles as she continues to write.

'I'm so happy I came, and that I had a place to come to. Thank you.'

'You'll be saying "please" and "sorry" next!' Bibiji shakes her head.

I laugh as I watch her writing, a bit faster than usual it seems.

'Which diary is that?'

'Same one.'

'What, 1958?' I lean over to confirm the date as she nods. 'But, Aunty, you've nearly finished it!'

'It will be finished before you go. You can take it with you.' She smiles and the mischievous tooth appears. I am moved and feel like hugging her. Instead, I wipe away a tear.

'What's there to cry about?'

'Nothing. Sorry, I didn't . . .'

161

'See! Didn't I tell you the sorry wouldn't be far behind?' The mischievous tooth has made its full appearance.

'Dear, dear Bibiji.' I get up and kiss her silver head.

'It is a joy, Meera, to see you well and more friends with yourself.'

Friends with myself! I think, as I walk over to pick a small branch of the pink bougainvillaeas and return with it to my chair. Friends with myself.

'I'm sure these bougainvillaeas are brighter – '

'Shh. Listen!' interrupts Bibiji as I sit down. 'Can you hear?'

'What? What in particular?' I ask. There are so many sounds around.

'That call? That's the sweet-potato man. We'll call him and have our sweet potatoes together. Minoo, Minoo! Maie!' she calls. Minoo pops out her head from the veranda as Bibiji fumbles in her purse for some money. 'Here take this and run along and get us some sweet potatoes. And get one for yourself too.' Minoo leaps off in delight, hitching her doll on her hip.

'You remember we were going to have sweet potatoes the day you came?'

'Yes, I remember.' I watch my great-aunt writing – and try not to blink my eyes, trying to imprint this moment into my consciousness as I wonder if Bibiji has always been friends with herself.

'Bibiji?' My tone is tentative.

'Yes, rani.' Hers definitive.

'There's something I'd like to ask you.'

'Ask it then, rani.'

I try to find the words. 'I'm not really sure if I should.'

'What sure, sure, should, should? Ask it anyway.'

'It's just that . . . I've often wondered . . . and never asked . . . and nobody knows . . . '

Bibiji lifts her head from her writing and looks at me directly, 'What is it, rani?'

'What I mean is . . . What's your story. The one that's the

family mystery and no one knows or dares to ask?'

She smiles . . . the reminiscing look . . . the glint of the tooth . . . the tell-tale signs of a good story are there. But she contains it, and resumes her writing. 'My story, eh! So you want to know my story.' She nods her head at her thoughts. 'Well there's a lot more to my story than the family mystery as they call it! It covers such a long time and so many changes. Changes which I have witnessed and participated in . . .' She looks up at me. 'Changes and upheavals and transformations in every sphere of life. And continuity too.' She continues to nod, 'Ah, yes! In the situation of women there have also been many changes, some I have even had a small share in making. Nowadays things are very different . . . there are many more opportunities, but still there is a lot of work that needs to be done. You young people must do that now, and are doing it.' She resumes her writing. She is thoughtful. The mischievous tooth flashes for an instant. 'It would take a long time to tell you all, but I will. I will tell you my story, rani – and many other stories – when you come back, which you'll do soon, I know that! It might just be for another holiday or an extended stay, but you'll be back and I'll be here and then I will tell you many stories and the so-called family mystery too.' She smiles to herself appearing to like the idea. 'You will then be the only living member in the family who will know! They all want to know, but none of them dares to ask.' Bibiji's face is all aglow with mischief – her tooth, her eyes, even her hair sparkling in the sunlight. As I am about to effuse delight and assure that I will come each year and every year from now on for as long as Bibiji is there, Minoo comes tearing in with the smoking-hot sweet potatoes, and Dr Shankar and Aunt Daya enter the gate.

'So, Meeru!' says Dr Shankar as Chandu arrives with napkins and tea and removes the remains of the snack. 'Tell me, then. Have you asked for your story as yet?'

'Story?' says Bibiji, looking at me uncertainly.

'What story?' asks Aunt Daya, in case she's missed something.

'Meera wants a story she can take back with her to London – a meaningful story. I told her she must ask you.'

'Acchaa! A story for Meera.' Bibiji smiles and returns to her writing. 'A story for Meera to take back with her.'

'I know which story,' says Aunt Daya, with defiance almost. 'I will tell it.'

Bibiji purses her lips, slightly irritated, but Dr Shankar pulls his chair forward and invites Aunt Daya to tell us.

'Shall I tell it, rani?' Aunt Daya asks me.

'Yes, Masi, please do,' I reply. Trying through my interest and tone to make up for my ungraciousness at the tale of the day before.

Aunt Daya starts, 'It is the story of a clay pot – which is given the power of speech and so it tells its own story. And it told: "Once I was part of the earth. Watered by the rains, warmed by the sun, at one with it all and at perfect peace. And then one day, a man came with a spade and, with its sharp blade, rooted me out and tore me apart from everything to which I belonged. What trouble! What pain! He then dumped me and left me in a heap in the corner to nurse my pain. I thought I'd be left alone, but no, there was more to come, for the next day he came with a hammer and beat me and beat me and beat me till I was crushed into a powder, and again he left me that way. This much I have suffered, I thought, now surely I will be left in peace." ' Aunt Daya stops. Her eyes have taken on a faraway look, almost as though she were reading the story from some distant horizon – or telling it to the sky.

' "The next day he came again. Mixed me with water, kneaded me and stamped on me until I became like putty in his hands. But even this was not enough, and my suffering had not ended, for then I was placed on a potter's wheel and there again I was beaten and turned round and round and round so as to become senseless almost as I was formed into a jar." ' Aunt Daya returns her attention to us, her audience, shaking her head as she recounts. ' "But still, my trials were not over. I was put to scorch in the sun by day, locked up at

164

night and then thrown into the fire to burn – oooh so terribly!" ' She shudders, increasingly identifying with the story. ' "So, I became a pot and was then taken to the bazaar, there people came and looked at me and fingered me and spurned me and banged me to test how good I was. Finally I was bought by someone who brought me to his home. There I was filled with water from the Ganga and placed on the altar with the flowers and incense, for the puja . . . and now," the pot said, "at last, I have found real peace and I understand everything I had to go through." ' Aunt Daya's face glows, her eyes shine and she emanates a sense of her being. We are all transfixed, for the story, which is clearly one most meaningful for her, has been invested with that special something else. She is still like I have never known her to be. Her voice is rich and full as she continues. 'Before, there was no pot. It was just part of everything and nothing and had to go through the pain and the fire to become a vessel, for only then could it be filled with the water of divine life.' Aunt Daya sits silent and still, as does everyone else. Bibiji is visibly moved.

'Daya, rani!' Bibiji's voice is deep and, oh, so low. 'You have told us this story like a gift.'

'It is a story I heard from Ma in Haridwar, some twenty years ago. Ma Anandamaee,' she tells me, in case I am unfamiliar with the saints of India. 'When she told it, I felt it was special for me, and then when I looked around, I saw it was for everyone, special for everyone.' Aunt Daya savours the memory silently, looking across at the same distant horizon.

As always, noise creeps into the silence, and yet, a silence remains. Aunt Daya glows, my discursive mind is suspended as I watch my aunt move with a light and sure step into the house to give the instructions for lunch. Bibiji follows her with a look – as though she were observing her for the first time. Slowly she picks up her book and pen and resumes her writing of 'ram ram ram . . . ' with renewed vigour.

'So, Meeru. Tell me. What did you think of your story?'

asks Dr Shankar.

'It was good. But then . . . what choices did the pot make, Uncle Shankar?'

Dr Shankar laughs heartily. 'Ahh, Meeru! One has to trust too. To trust is also a choice.'

Thirty

My dear friend,

It is my last day and I have woken up early. Outside it is not yet dawn and sounds are only just beginning to stir the silence. It must be the 'amritvela' that Aunt Daya was telling me about – the time of nectar, the time just before the first light begins to dispel the darkness of the night, when the sun has risen but cannot as yet be seen. That most auspicious time, when, it is said, the mind is sharpest, most receptive. How nice that I should have woken up at the amritvela on my last day.

I am all packed and ready – though there is still the whole day ahead of me as my plane doesn't leave till the early hours of tomorrow morning. I finished everything last night so that my last day would be free of rush. But there wasn't much to do, and not much to pack. My luggage is much lighter than when I came – I haven't done much shopping and all the clothes that crammed it full have been distributed. But it's not only my luggage that feels lighter – I, too, feel that I have shed a weight. I realised it after the fever had left, but now my whole being confirms it – as if a whole new and clear space had been created within me. These last few days have been both peaceful and pleasant and filled with stories. Following Dr Shankar's advice, I stayed at home. Ashok, Bibiji's protegé bought me the sandalwood visiting cards for Martin and a local shop sent over a selection of embroidered pyjama kurta sets from which I chose one, also for Martin, and yesterday Radha and Aunt Pushpa came to say goodbye and brought a lovely silver pendant of Saraswati on a chain for Maya.

Within me and around me there has been a subtle transformation. Since she told her story of the clay pot, Aunt Daya walks around with a new confidence in her step and Bibiji eyes her with an almost respectful look. Dr Shankar talked to me about trust and though I do not quite understand all that he meant, I am aware that a feeling akin to that is growing within me. Throughout my stay I have searched – for questions, for answers, for clues that would show me the way . . . Now, paradoxically, I am leaving and feeling I've arrived, and my questions have dissolved leaving me unburdened and light, almost as though I'd found whatever it was. Maybe that's trust. Or maybe it's amritvela! When the first light sets a new perspective, as yesterday dissolves and tomorrow becomes today! There is an amritvela everywhere! . . .

Aunt Daya tiptoes into my room but on seeing the light on and me writing, walks over briskly to my bed.

'So, you're up and working?' she asks.

'No, Masi, I'm sleeping and dreaming!'

'Good!' she replies. 'Here, take this!' She holds out a slice of apple, and seeing that my hands are full with pen and book, she pops it into my mouth and sits down on the bed.

'So. You're all packed?'

'All packed.'

'Just one case?'

'Just one case.'

'That's good. And what are you writing there?'

'Oh, just – a letter.'

'A letter? Who to? You'll be there soon now.' She peers over to have a look. 'You write letters in a book? Is it a special book for writing letters?'

'Yes, Aunty,' I laugh. 'It's a special book for writing

letters!'

'Then what do you do? Tear the pages out?'

'Well, no. Not exactly. The pages stay in the book, because you see . . . I write the letters to the book.'

'To the book?' She looks at me questioningly.

'Well . . . through the book to whoever I want to write to. I started it when Ma and Papa died.' Aunt Daya looks at me with full attention. 'It happened quite by chance. I had this very nice book.'

'This same one?'

'No, a different one. I needed someone to talk to, so I picked up this book and wrote – a letter to an imaginary friend.'

Aunt Daya nods her head knowingly. 'I know, I know. I had a little murthi like that. I'd talk to it like a friend – whatever kind of friend I wanted it to be – my father, my mother – anything. And always I would carry it with me. I had a little pocket bag tucked in my bodice and always it was there.'

'And now too?'

'No. Not now.' She shakes her head, remembering, as I wait for her to continue. 'Some years ago I went on a pilgrimage – with your mother – to the Kumbh Mela. That's a very special pilgrimage which takes place only once every twelve years. Thousands and thousands of people go. We go to Allahbad, where the two rivers meet – the Ganga and the Jamuna – and everyone bathes there. Always there are big, big crowds. Your mother and I tied the ends of our saris together so we wouldn't lose each other! Did you know that?'

I shake my head.

'Well, we did. Of course, it can be dangerous because if one person falls, then the others fall and the crowd tramples them. You've never been on a pilgrimage, huh?'

'No. It doesn't sound very inviting for my taste either. But you were telling me about your murthi,' I remind my aunt, who is digressing into other memories.

169

'Ah, yes. We went to bathe in the river, which sometimes has very heavy currents, and it was only when we came back that I realised that the murthi had gone. Now, how it got out of my bodice, I don't know! Under here it was.' Aunt Daya places her hand below her left breast. 'But it did. It was gone. The river had taken it away!' Her tone is light.

'Weren't you upset?'

'At first I was. Then the next morning when I woke up for my early prayers . . . '

'At amritvela?'

'Oh, yes. Always. After I had said my prayers I understood. Gangaji had taken the murthi away from me because I no longer needed it. Instead the murthi was now in me . . . ' she looks out through the window at the distant horizon, '. . . and around me.'

I put aside my book and sit up to throw my arms around the frail frame of my aunt. 'Dear Aunt Daya! You're so sweet! And I do love you! Next time I come I shall come with you to Haridwar and get up every morning at amritvela!'

'Huh!' she retorts, untangling herself from my embrace. 'You young people don't believe in all these things!'

'So what. You do. And I can watch you.'

'I won't bring you tea this morning. Bibiji wants you to have it with her in her room. Chandu will be bringing it soon.'

Aunt Daya gets up and unlocks one of the cupboards in my room. 'A few days after you go, I too will go back to the hills,' she says as she rummages through the cupboard. Pulling out a little packet she returns to my bedside. 'This is for you. It's a shawl. See.' She pulls it out. 'It's finer than silk, warmer than wool and so soft you can only know if you feel it.'

'But, Masi!'

'Don't argue. It was given to me and now I'm giving it to you.'

'But really! You keep it. It's much more useful to you. I don't need it.'

170

'Silly girl. When you have it you'll see you need it. Take it.'

'Then you must tell me of something I can bring you when I next come that you'll need if you have it!'

'That's silly-style talk. You just listen to your elders. To accept a gift, is also . . . giving.'

'Thank you, Masi. It's beautiful. Thank you.'

'No! No "thank you sorry" business! Hut theri!' She rises in mock indignation. 'Always teasing your old masi! Go to Bibiji now. I can hear Chandu . . . '

Aunt Daya leaves the room in her same hurried manner, but with that new confidence in her step. Could all that have changed simply through the telling of a story! Or is it my vision that has changed, like in that poem – 'the altering eye alters all . . . ' Who wrote it? I must remember to ask Martin. Maybe poems work in the same way as stories and one remembers fragments when one needs to! What was it Dr Shankar said? Don't try and always understand – just include. Understanding will grow. Maybe that's trust. Dear India! Continuity and change! Stories and dust!

'Now are you going, raniji, and you still haven't let me give you your massage.' Maie greets me as I enter the room. I smile at her as she grins me her toothless grin and closes all the jars of cream.

'Next time. Soon,' I reply.

'Yes. Soon,' returns Bibiji. 'Come, baby, sit, sit. Pour yourself some tea. It's freshly made.'

'I'll go now and get the flowers,' says Maie heaving herself up and picking up all the jars as she does so. 'I'll string some up for your hair too, raniji.'

'What, the same flowers as for the gods?'

'Why not?' she returns.

Bibiji smiles as I drink my tea. 'I have arranged for a taxi to take you to the airport. I called Bhagwan Das and he has said he will drive you himself. He's absolutely reliable. I've known him since Lahore – he was only a boy then.'

'Lahore, eh!'

'Yes. Lahore. His family ran a tonga business.'

'The old days in Old Lahore.'

'Yes, yes,' Bibiji smiles. 'Old Lahore.'

'You know, last night as I was packing I remembered a story. I probably didn't get it quite right, but I thought it sort of suited me!' I laugh. Bibiji raises her eyebrows to indicate that I continue. 'You know that one about the man who loses his key in his house and then goes out to look for it and can't find it anywhere and gets lost looking?'

Bibiji looks at me and laughs.

'I've got it all wrong, haven't I?'

'I'm laughing because I can remember your father telling that same story to someone some years ago, in this very house.'

'It must have come to me from the dust then. Tell it to me though.'

'Okay, okay. But first call Chandu and then we can have more tea.'

Before I can do so, Chandu appears with a kettle and refills the pot – all the while delivering a smile.

'The story goes that once a passer-by saw a man searching for something on the ground and asked him what he was looking for and the man replied that he'd lost his key. So the passer-by stopped to help him find it and both of them searched around in the ground. After a while the passer-by asked the man: "But where exactly did you lose it?" And the man replied, "In the house". So the passer-by said, "But then if you lost it in the house, why are you looking for it out here?" "Ah, but you see," replied the man, "there's more light here and my house is all dark!" '

I can just imagine my father telling this story . . .

'This morning Aunt Daya insisted on giving me a shawl. It's silly really.'

'Na, na. You keep it.'

'But it's much more useful to her, here, than to me.'

'You must try and keep it carefully and give it to Maya. It's

172

the shahtús.'

'The shahtús?'

'Yes. They're very rare and valuable now.'

'I didn't realise that.'

'And also,' continues Bibiji with a smile, ' . . . it has a story.'

'A story?'

'Yes, that's Daya's story. But the shawl used to be my mother's, that's to say, Daya's grandmother and your great-grandmother. Every cool season she would wear it and everyone would admire it, it was such a fine shahtús. Also, apart from a few trinkets, it is the only personal possession of my mother's that survived the Partition. At that time, many of us were out of Lahore, Daya was up in the hills in Dalhousie, and those left behind had to leave in a hurry and everything was abandoned. Many of us never really believed that we would have to leave, you see. We'd lived side by side for years.' Bibiji looks thoughtful and sips her tea.

'In any case, for a long time no one knew if the shahtús had been saved – because Daya never gave a straight answer.'

'Did she tell you?'

'I never asked her, but some years ago she told me.'

'So, it's a real treasure!'

Bibiji smiles. 'I'm glad she has given it to you.'

'Why me?'

'Why not, rani? Why not you?'

'It's like inheriting the mantle of a tradition from which I am uprooted and of which I know nothing.'

Bibiji smiles. 'Well, it's Daya's to give. Like it was my mother's to give and she gave it to Daya.'

'Was there a reason?'

'That's Daya's story, rani. It's for her to tell it.'

'I was thinking about it these last few days actually. Daya Masi must have quite a story of her own to tell.'

'Oh yes!' replies Bibiji as she leans down to the lower tier of her table to find something. 'Here. Take this. It is the book you wanted. It's completed . . . '

173

'Bibi–'

'Na, na, don't say. That you should want it is thanks enough. What is it anyway? Just an old book.'

I turn the pages of the diary in my hand. 'But such a nice one! 1958! What happened in 1958?'

'1958. That's the year I built this house?'

'This house?' I look around at the walls of the room. 'If Martin can come with me the next time, we'll paint this room up for you.'

'You don't want to come here and start painting rooms.'

'No, really! You get really good rollers and go whoosh, whoosh.'

Bibiji laughs. 'I don't know about any whooshes and whos. You come and stay and enjoy. This house is okay as it is. Come. Enough talking for this morning. Go and get ready now yourself. Give me my stick and then send Daya to me and see why Maie is taking so long, call Minoo and send her.'

In my room, as I get ready for my bath I imagine how nice the room would look with a coat of brilliant white emulsion – and in the bathroom, a sea green or maybe even an ice blue to give a feeling of cool in the summer, which I can only imagine as I splash the hot water over me. I could come next time in the summer . . .

Back in my room I notice the string of pink bougainvillaeas that Maie has put on my dressing table next to Aunt Daya's makeshift shrine – where the oil lamp has also been lit. I pull a few flowers off the string and place them between the leaves of Bibiji's book, before enfolding it carefully in the shawl and placing the treasures in my hand luggage. Behind me the oil lamp splutters, drawing my attention to it. I walk over and inspect the familiar objects.

'Aha, ram ram, rani, you're ready. That's good. We'll have breakfast together. What's that you're doing?' Aunt Daya walks over to join me and seeing the statue in my hand announces, 'That's Parvati, the Devi, the Great Goddess. She is also Uma, and Durga, and Kali and Ambika. She has many forms. She is beautiful, gentle, timeless, terrible, the mother and saviour of the world. You take her with you, rani. This murthi belonged to your mother.'

'No, Masi. It's not for me.'

'Of course it's for you. It's yours.'

'No, no, please.' To my aunt's look of dismay I add, 'What I mean is, let her stay here for when I come back – next time. I don't need to carry her back to London. In any case you'll look after her much better than I would. But there is something I'd like you to do for me.'

'What's that, rani? What can I do?'

'This book of mine.'

'What, your letter-writing book?' she says on seeing it in my hand.

'Yes. My letter-writing book. I'd like you to take it with you . . . and put it in the Ganga for me.' I hand it to her.

'But why do you want to do that? Why do you want to put it in the Ganga? And it's still got good pages in it.' My aunt flicks through the pages of the book. 'You can still write more in it.'

'I don't need to . . . '

'You mean you won't do any more writing?'

'I don't know. Maybe. Then I'll get a new book and fill it with all the stories I've been told and that you are going to tell me when I come back.'

'But you can do all that here,' Aunt Daya insists. 'There's lots of good pages. Such a waste.'

'You can cut the good pages out and put the rest into the water. It's like with your little murthi. I no longer need it – at least, not like before. And if Gangaji has it, that understanding will remain with me.'

Aunt Daya smiles. 'Accha. I'll do it. But I'll tear the good pages out. It's very bad to waste. Such nice paper too. I'll give it to some children for drawing. You nearly ready for breakfast, rani?'

'I'll just do my hair, put Maie's flowers in, and come.'

Aunt Daya makes to leave the room, and then suddenly

stops at the half-opened door as if remembering something.
'Rani.'

'Yes, Masi.'

'You remember . . . when I told you . . . that it was a great gift to be born a human being . . . '

'And not some creepy-crawly creature. Yes, I remember.'

'You laughed then, too, rani, but it is something to thank for. A human being can grow, can change, understand . . . discriminate. That's the great gift!'

Thirty-one

After the rush and noise of the airport, the plane is calm, cocooned, with everybody gratefully settling into their nests. Outside it is still dark, but soon it will be the amritvela once again – a brief time quivering between the 'kal' of yesterday and the 'kal' of tomorrow. Maybe even for an instant they are all one – yesterday, today and tomorrow. Ah, amritvela! The coming of the light to shed new perspectives on life. Surely, travelling from east to west, I will ride with the sun, and so ride through a long dawning of amritvelas! A long time of nectar! I smile at the idea and close my eyes to savour it. Yes, there is an amritvela everywhere – and every day!

The plane rumbles and roars in readiness. As it flies up, the lights are dimmed and we are away. Through the window I watch the city disappear below us, flickering away into the distance. The air hostess walks down the aisle offering blankets. I refuse mine. Instead, from the bag by my side I carefully take out and unfold the shahtús – so soft, so warm, so light as to be almost weightless. And it smells – yes – it smells of India. Dear Aunt Daya, you are quite right. Now that I have it, I do need it; it is just what I need.

I am on my way home. From my home in the East, to my home in the West, safely through my space – my home in the clouds. Yes, I have come – and am going – home. For now I can sleep, safely on the plane. For a plane is always safe: whichever way I am going, it always carries me home.

Glossary

aam papad	mango pancakes
aloo	potato
bania	shopkeeper
bas	enough
Baisakhi	spring festival
baraat	bridegroom's wedding party
bhabiji	respected sister-in-law
bhai	brother
bhaloo	bear
behn, bhenji	sister, respected sister
bibi	woman
burri	big
chamchas	literally, spoons; figuratively, stooges
dahi	yogurt
devi	goddess
dhania	coriander
dhobi	washerman
Divali	festival of lights

durbar	audience chamber
gulaam	knave, fool, servant
habshi	black
jawans	foot soldiers
laddus	type of sweet
lakh	unit of 100,000
maie	woman
mala	rosary
mali	gardener
masi	aunt: mother's sister
mandir	temple
meri	mine, my
mochi	shoemaker
murthi	image, figurine
namaste	a greeting
paat	prayer
paneer	cheese
prasaad	consecrated food
puja	prayer
ram	that which dwells in all
rasgullas	type of sweet
rani, raniji	queen
roti	bread
sandesh	type of sweet
sanyasin	someone who renounces worldly things in

	search of the spiritual life
sat pathi	seven steps taken round the fire at weddings
seva	caring, looking after people as a form of worship
shabash	well done
shahtús	very fine wool, softer than cashmere
tonga	horse-drawn carriage

Ravinder Randhawa
A Wicked Old Woman

'Forget fiction. Real life is where the drama lies.'

Stick-leg-shuffle-leg-shuffle: decked out with NHS specs and Oxfam coat, Kulwant masquerades behind her old woman's disguise, taking life or leaving it as she feels inclined, seeking new adventures or venturing back into her past.

Divorced from her husband, disapproved of by her sons, mistrusted by their wives, Kuli makes real contact through a jigsaw of meetings in the present: with Bahadur the Punjabi punk who dusts her down after a carefully calculated fall, with Caroline, her gregarious friend from school days, who watched over her dizzy romance with 'Michael the archangel', with Maya the myopic who can't see beyond her weeping heart, and with Shanti who won't see, whose eyes will remain closed till her runaway daughter returns to the fold.

A sharply observed first novel set in an Asian community in a British city – a witty and confident piece of work from a talented new writer.

Fiction. £4.95 paperback
ISBN: 0 7043 4078 X
£12.95 hardback
ISBN: 0 7043 5032 7

Suniti Namjoshi
The Conversations of Cow

Suniti and Bhadravati disagree about almost everything – which is hardly surprising as Suniti is an average middle of the road lesbian separatist and Bhadravati is a Brahmin lesbian cow, goddess of a thousand faces and a thousand manifestations.

Suniti has been unlucky in love and thinks she is becoming a misogynist. So it's only natural that when Bhadravati transforms herself into a woman, Suniti decides to become a goldfish (or perhaps a poodle or another cow). When Bhadravati manifests herself as a man, things can only get worse.

Fiction   Paperback/£2.95
ISBN: 0 7043 3979 X
Hardback   £7.95
ISBN: 0 7043 2870 4